MURDER BOY

by Bryon Quertermous

"Quertermous has made the bold decision to add a tremendous injection of gallows humor to the traditionally dead serious crime fiction arena. Don't let the lighter tone fool you though. Woven in amidst the antics is a subtle journey of self-discovery, as well as a rather biting, and accurate, commentary about the perils of tying one's identity to one's ambition. The end result of it all is a wonderfully refreshing change of pace, and an authorial voice that immediately sets itself apart from the pack."

—*Florida Times-Union*

"I found MURDER BOY disturbing in a GOOD way, the best possible way. It's hilarious, yet incredibly aware of its own twisted reality. Personally, I don't know of another book like it. Saying something is such-and-such "with heart" is a big meta-joke, but I thought MURDER BOY truly was a black comedy with heart."

—Laura Lippman, *New York Times* bestselling author of *Hush Hush* and *What the Dead Know*

"Bryon Quertermous has the thing that every writer strives for and many never find: a truly unique voice. His writing is crisp and clean, his storytelling sense is honed, but it's the voice that holds the magic. The balance of the comedic and the dramatic in his work is a rare treat, reading like a deliciously blood-soaked crime novel rewritten by Christopher Moore. Try the first sentence of MURDER BOY, and then tell me if I'm wrong."

—Michael Koryta, *New York Times* bestselling author of *Those Who Wish Me Dead*

"Quertermous gives Dominick an almost continual output of insightful, and often times laugh out loud funny, narration that stands apart from the pack. Clearly influenced by Duane Swierczynski and Victor Gischler, Bryon Quertermous makes his debut novel MURDER BOY stand apart and on its own."

—*CrimeSpree Magazine*

"Bryon Quertermous's MURDER BOY is chock-full of crackling dialogue, whirlwind pacing and the most sociopaths per capita of any book I've read in a long time. (I mean that in a good way.) It's dark, brutal, and irresistible."

—Kelly Braffet, author of *Save Yourself*

"Forget the debate over MFA vs. NYC raging in bookish circles right now. Bryon Quertermous fires a shotgun blast through that false dichotomy with his crackling debut novel MURDER BOY, as much a violent romp and action-packed tale as it is a sobering look at thwarted literary dreams, the corrosive results of envy and jealousy, and finding courage and mettle close to home and heart."

—Sarah Weinman, editor of *Women Crime Writers* and *Troubled Daughters, Twisted Wives*

"Bryon Quertermous has created a witty, gritty thriller. Equal parts Elmore Leonard and WONDER BOYS, this book is a winner. With a voice that carries you and a pace that pushes you, this is a book you can't miss."

—Dave White, Shamus Award–nominated author of the Jackson Donne series

"Rough and raw and fast and furious and genuinely funny, with a dizzying array of villains and a hefty dose of madcap adventure, Bryon Quertermous's love letter to the crime fiction genre, MURDER BOY, is an awesome debut from a talented, assured voice. MURDER BOY is a winner."

—J.T. Ellison, *New York Times* bestselling author of *When Shadows Fall*

"MURDER BOY is at once dark, irreverent, and laugh-out-loud funny—a breakneck tale that manages to both send up and pay homage to the tropes of the crime genre. I'd expect nothing less from the twisted mind of Bryon Quertermous."

—Chris Holm, author of *The Killing Kind*

"Within a few chapters of MURDER BOY, I started hearing Goodis in the background, but with a postmodern wink and nudge. Quertermous has something to tell us, and I'm damn sure going to listen. Keep an eye out. This guy's got the voice."

—Anthony Neil Smith, author of the Billy Lafitte series and founder of *Plots with Guns*

"One part manic and one part meta, MURDER BOY is as much a meditation on love, loss, dashed hopes and second chances as it is a crime-filled, gonzo-pulp fever dream fueled by booze and bodily fluids."

—*The Maine Suspect*

"Quertermous has created a work which exists simultaneously as both a classic example of the noir thriller and as a unique dark comedic attack against the hypocrisy of academia."

—BOLO Books

# RIOT LOAD

Bryon Quertermous

The following is a work of fiction. Names, characters, places, events and incidents are either the product of the author's imagination or used in an entirely fictitious manner. Any resemblance to actual persons, living or dead, is entirely coincidental.


Cover and jacket design by Adrijus Guscia
Interior designed and formatted by E.M. Tippetts Book Designs

ISBN 978-1-940610-68-9
eISBN: 978-1-943818-12-9
Library of Congress Control Number: 2016934068

First trade paperback edition June 2016 by Polis Books, LLC
1201 Hudson Street
Hoboken, NJ 07030
www.PolisBooks.com

POLIS BOOKS

To the booksellers who hosted me for events at their wonderful indie bookstores for *Murder Boy*:

McKenna Jordan, John Kwiatkowski, and Sally Woods a
Murder by the Book

Barbara Peters, David Hunenberg, Patrick Millikin, and
Jeff Kronenfeld at The Poisoned Pen

Otto Penzler and Ian Kern from The Mysterious Booksho

Robin Agnew and James Agnew from Aunt Agatha's.

Thank you doesn't even begin to cover it.

RIOT LOAD

I was two hours into my thirty-minute lunch break and taking in a baseball game on a stuffy mid-July day in Detroit when it occurred to me that getting everything I ever wanted was the worst thing that could have happened to me.

"That one," I said to the hot dog vendor, pointing to a short black woman across the way.

He nodded and handed me a sausage and a can of Diet Coke.

"Just once or more than that?"

He shrugged and took the five-dollar bill I handed him. I handed him another five. And then another.

"Three times," he said. "Once with another woman. Younger. White."

"Both were wearing hospital badges?"

He nodded again. I didn't have any more money but I had what I needed. My coworkers had been spying on me. I took my time finishing my sausage and my Diet Coke, trying to enjoy the game and the atmosphere. After the game, I was walking back to my office at the university medical center around the corner when I saw a police cruiser following me. It wasn't unusual to see police cars around that part of town, especially on game day, but this wasn't a Detroit Police Department cruiser, it was one of the nicer, shinier Detroit State University cruisers. I sighed and slowed down.

"Got time for a friend?" Lindsey Buckingham asked.

"Gotta get back to work," I said. "Can I come and—"

"Bullshit," she said. "I've been watching you for a bit and you never—"

"Why have you been following me?"

"Get in. They got me on a tighter leash and I can't be roaming like I used to."

I got in and had a rush of emotion.

I was never sure how to tell people the story of what happened to me. I worked out most of my emotions writing my first novel, but the actual day-to-day trauma and psychological damage still popped up at the damndest times. Like right then.

Wow.

So short of breath.

"I need a favor," Lindsey said.

I tried to open the door, but even a campus cruiser had the back door child locks to keep prisoners from escaping so the door didn't open and I stayed in the car.

Running out of breath.

Jesus. So hot.

I looked out the window and saw we were back to the hospital where I worked. My breathing returned to normal and I felt less boxed in. Staying in the car with Lindsey was better than going back to work and facing my conspiring coworkers.

"I can take the rest of the day off if you need me," I said. "I *do* owe you."

Lindsey turned as far around as she could to face me and poked her index finger toward my face.

"You need to go back to work and be the best employee you can be."

"That's your favor? Be a good employee?"

"We'll talk more tomorrow. This is going to be rough on you but like you said. You owe me."

When I was out of the car Lindsey yelled at me again.

"And don't tell your wife about this."

Right. My wife.

• • •

I MARRIED Posey Wade after her brother was murdered.

It started kind of as a joke. We'd been classmates and teaching partners during my last year of grad school for creative writing. When Parker Farmington, my thesis advisor and academic arch nemesis failed me and wouldn't sign the paperwork for me to graduate, it was Posey's naked shoulder I cried on in a hot tub while confessing my secret desire to kidnap Parker. Instead of ratting me out to the cops or to Parker, she took pity on me and put me in touch with a guy she knew who also wanted to kidnap Parker.

I don't want to get into all of the details of what happened, I still have nightmares and panic attacks regularly because of it, but her brother ended up dead and so did the guy she hooked me up with. But rather than pull away from me, she pulled me closer.

We went out a few times after she lost a beer pong bet to me and we fooled around casually for a bit but then she got pregnant and it wasn't much of a joke. Posey took it well, which surprised me, but what surprised me even more was how well *I* took it. My first girlfriend out of high school got pregnant a week after graduation while we were both still under the brainwashing spells of our religious upbringing. I bought a shitty ring that I gave to her in a half-assed proposal and took a stable, but shitty, job as a telephone electrician to pay the bills. For a long time I resented the sacrifices I had made to accommodate the situation and believed they held me back from achieving my true destiny as a writer (spoiler alert: turns out my lazy attitude toward the world and underdeveloped writing talent were the actual culprits). It was a mark of my selfishness and immaturity that I viewed the miscarriage of that pregnancy as my escape from the situation and a fresh start of my writing life.

Hopefully I'm not that much of a twit these days. After fighting and scheming so hard for an opportunity to have the freedom and money to do nothing but write, it only took me about three months of that life for me to get lazy and devolve into a structure-less void with no real purpose or aim. I spent those three months writing my novel, *Blood Boy* (a riff on my grad school nickname), and when the novel was done, I was done. I put everything I ever learned, experienced, read, imagined, and wished for into that book and seemed happy for that to be the only thing I would ever write.

The book was published by a digital publisher out of the UK, and the day I cashed the second half of the advance check I stopped going to class, stopped teaching, stopped writing, and started watching a lot of television on DVD. Just about the time the university came calling for their fellowship money back, I moved in with Posey, who had jumped head first into keeping her brother's bail bonds business afloat. She fired most of the bail recovery agents her brother used, and after a month-long training class in Nevada she bought a gun, a Taser, and a lifetime supply of pepper spray and plastic wrist ties and became a bounty hunter. I had fun playing house and even went out and got my own self a job. My extensive writing training was a perfect fit for mindless clerical work and the money and benefits were good but I still found it hard to get excited for life, and that's how I found myself at a baseball game piecing together exactly how my bitchy coworkers were spying on me. For the first time in a long time I was excited to get to work the next day. Excited to see what was going to happen next.

I showed up at work the next morning to find an HR rep and my two coworkers waiting for me in the conference room. The meeting wasn't a surprise but my reaction to it was. Had it happened a day earlier I would have been on the defensive and looking to be a manipulative prick and probably gotten myself fired. But I was intrigued enough by Lindsey's favor and the caveat that I do anything possible to keep my job, that I went into the meeting with my most contrite face on and played the apologetic father-to-be and bought myself a second chance. At least with HR.

"You're a liar and we're going to prove it," Cammy Tate, the nastier of the two, said to me on the way back to the office suite.

I kept my mouth shut and tried not to flip her off. She was a thirty-year-old Ivy League graduate with two master's degrees and a patent for something involving the drive train on race cars, but thanks to the rotten Michigan economy and the sexist world of academic medicine, she was nothing more than a secretary who made $10,000 less than I did and worked ten times as hard. Around lunch time being a good employee was starting to get exhausting and I was wondering how I could last the entire day when my boss waved me into the conference room. I was genuinely surprised for once and had no idea what I had done.

Sarah Janus was a squat Asian woman with scarred, leathery skin and a paranoid demeanor that hinted at a rough life prior to joining our office. It also made judging her age nearly impossible. On casual glance she would appear to be in her fifties or sixties, but every once in a while she would drop a pop culture reference, such as her recent conversation about how underappreciated *Dawson's Creek* was in its day, that made me wonder if she was closer to my age.

"Shared services wants you in the sperm lab," she said with a straight face.

"They want me what?"

She shrugged and didn't even seem to be on the verge of cracking a smile. It wasn't an odd request—shared services was a stupid program that resulted in some really stupid day-long placements for me—but the sperm lab was a new one.

"It's still the cancer center," she said. "Something about prostate patients. You know, I didn't pay too much attention to it once they mentioned the...you know, the location."

"I take the bus here," I said. "Is there a stop at the—"

"It's in this complex," she said. "I think it will be good for you to get out of here for a while, you know, with *those* two out for you again."

"Yeah, okay."

Sperm lab. Well, I certainly didn't see that coming. In the time I'd been with the Detroit State University Cancer Center as a medical administrative assistant my job had changed three times, my boss had changed twice, and now they were trying this shared services nonsense that made all administrative employees eligible for placement anywhere in the cancer center. I'd been placed in several different offices, but they were all administrative offices with the same oak and glass décor that all of the department chairs demanded and the same basic layout and the same group of bitter middle-aged former housewives running the show.

As a male I was always viewed with a healthy bit of skepticism and usually found myself living down to their worst expectations. But a lab was different. I wasn't sure if it was good different, but it was different enough to excite me and I started wondering if I'd be inspired to reinvigorate my dormant science fiction writing passion. Early in my writing career I'd been obsessed with Isaac Asimov, Ray Bradbury, and Michael Crichton and how they mixed real-world science into their fantastic stories. This was also during the brief period in my life when I believed anything was possible and harbored dreams of being an engineer or computer programmer despite lacking the needed math skills to even understand the recruiting brochures for the computer club.

I felt excited enough to eat healthy and take a walk during my lunch. It was sunny and breezy and I had a light step until I saw a familiar uniformed police officer heading my way. I kept my happy walk and my happy demeanor until Lindsey said,

"Have you started your new assignment yet?"

"How did you know—"

"You're not the only one who owes me favors. Have you started yet?"

"No. I was having lunch first."

"Good. I need you to be aware from the beginning and if you suddenly start looking aware after they meet you it will look suspicious when…well, I'm getting ahead of myself."

"Why do I need to be aware? What does this all have to do with a sperm bank?"

"I just need you to scope a few things out for me," she said.

"What kind of things?"

"Location mostly and escape routes."

Oh shit. This wasn't going to turn out well.

"Escape routes? I can't break any more laws."

"It'll be fine," she said. "That sample is mine anyway. I don't care what your wife says."

Double shit. Jesus. My mind was already taking what it knew and drawing some very creepy conclusions.

"What is yours?" I asked.

"The sample," she said. "You know he had cancer, right? That's why he shaved his head. I always liked the look but—"

"No," I said. "This is creepy and gross and…Jesus, I'm married to his sister."

I'd never fully understood Lindsey's relationship with Titus Wade. She'd explained it to me a few times—something about Titus being the first guy she had sex with after making a pact with God related to her surviving a sexual assault—but the details never stuck. When he was alive, Lindsey's sole driving force in life was convincing Titus Wade he was her soul mate, and now that he was dead, she'd gone all-in on pursuing his remaining…essence…with the same passion.

"You're the only one who can do this. I tried and they… well, that doesn't matter. You owe me."

"I'm *married* to his *sister,*" I said.

"You owe me. Titus Wade owes me. He promised me and that bitch sister of his—"

"That's my wife. Jesus. I can't even—"

"I want a baby. I want *his* baby. But he's dead."

"And you want me to steal his sperm sample?"

"You *owe* me."

Lindsey gave me instructions, but I couldn't really process much of it because I was still trying to wrap my mind around how creepy and wrong the situation was that she was putting me in.

The woman who saved my ass from jail had a weird crush on my wife's brother the bounty hunter who, before he was murdered by a serial killer obsessed with baseball and my training as a writer, deposited a sperm sample at the cancer center where he was secretly being treated for prostate cancer in case he ever wanted to have kids. As executor of her brother's estate, Posey had control over all her brother's assets, even the icky ones, and, according to Lindsey, she had no interest in turning it over for procreation.

I tried to use my training as a writer to consider all of the viewpoints and find validity in them rather than immediately seeing Lindsey's request as an affront to my wife and her family affairs, but failed on almost all accounts. The one area I did not fail in was keeping my job. I survived the rest of the day, and managed to take a few notes and get a few pictures of the lab and its surrounding environs on my iPhone before I left. But I was going to have to get my head straight if I was going to survive longer than a half day in that environment.

My first thought was to try and talk to Posey and see if I could casually push her toward a peaceful resolution, but she was in a foul mood when she got home so we ignored each other and went to bed early. And it went on like that for almost a week. I was about ready to abandon it all when I ended up in a strip club with two boneheads Posey was looking for and things started looking up.

The second day at work after Lindsey ambushed me had been awful and the third was even worse. It was awkward and I hated the work and I hated the lab environment. Nobody spoke English, everything was cold all the time, and everything smelled like bleach or formaldehyde. But by the fourth day, I pulled my head out of my ass enough to notice I was in the perfect position for a reconnaissance mission. I had no direct supervisor; my work for the day was easily done in under an hour if I tried really hard, and nobody paid attention to me. I had free range of the entire floor and was able to put together a pretty detailed plan of attack for Lindsey, but I was hesitant to turn it over to her because I hadn't yet reconciled Posey's stake in the whole matter. At one point I even wrote out our marriage vows on a piece of scrap paper to look for a loophole in the wording. No luck.

To help atone for my impending betrayal, I was putting more effort into our life at home, trying to make Posey's life easier and our relationship stronger. Housework has never been my strong suit, and Posey is even worse than I am, so there were plenty of things around the house that had piled up. I did the dishes, washed and dried a load of laundry (I would never in my life have enough ambition to put away laundry), and organized her gun safe. For a brief moment I considered cooking dinner as well, and even fell down a few recipe rabbit holes on Pinterest before realizing neither Posey nor I cooked because we liked takeout far more than we liked eating at home. I made a collage of her favorite takeout menus and put it on the kitchen table where she would see it when she came in.

I'm sure she saw right through it, but she was swamped at work and didn't have the luxury of rejecting my offer. I also assumed she was testing me as well. She'd made no secret of her desire for me to work with her. Any time I complained about a crappy job or writer's block or the lack of decent movies in the theater these days, she'd spin it as a sign from the universe that I was meant to be a bounty hunter with her.

"We're the same, you and me," she would say. "Romantics, lovers of literature, of conflict, of random socially inappropriate nudity. The perfect people for this life."

She'd go on and on about the abundance of under-educated and over-muscled thugs in the business and how it needed new blood like me to gain respectability, and I'd think about it and be swayed by her argument briefly before bringing up the point that always shut the argument down. White guy. Black city. Detroit had enough problems; the last thing the city needed was another white do-gooder looking to take young black men back to jail. There was also the very real possibility that anyone I tried to capture and take to jail would capture me instead. The one time I tried to capture my thesis advisor, three people ended up dead and I spent a significant amount of time in my own trunk.

But unrelenting in her assault on my career passivity, we were having dinner and watching *Wheel of Fortune* one evening and she said, "I've got some guys I need you to find. It involves a strip club."

She seemed genuinely excited for me, but there was another issue at play more volatile to me than the race angle. I was still having nightmares from the last time I tried to play bounty hunter. She knew about the nightmares and the panic attacks, having calmed me down in the middle of most of them, but she kept trying to get me to move forward and work through them. It was an ideological chasm between the way she grew up and the way I'd grown up. I was prone to over-analyzing and taking medicine to help me deal with illness and trauma and she just barreled through it all and didn't have any patience for my more cerebral approach.

"I don't know," I said. "I've got this new job and they just moved me—"

"To a lab where you don't have shit to do all day. You were just complaining last night—"

"Fine. No. I'm glad to help. Is it…I mean do I have to…"

"It's a following job," she said. "I'm not asking you to take them down."

"Oh." My face relaxed and I smiled. "Okay."

• • •

I'VE NEVER been comfortable in strip clubs but I was finding myself in them to a rather absurd degree lately, and this latest club did nothing to build my interest in the art of sweat- and flesh gyrating–based entertainment. It was a dive bar with a neon green paint job, no visible signage, and an atmosphere that made me wonder if there was an airborne form of hepatitis I could catch. I waited ten minutes to pay my cover while the doorman (that sounds way too fancy but this guy was a scrawny little turd of a man I could never bring myself to call a bouncer, so doorman it is) argued with another guy about the paint job.

"Same fucking color," the other guy said. "*Exact* fucking color. How does that happen?"

"I call a guy, I tell him to paint it bright, and you run over my sign with a truck," the doorman said. "How does *that* happen?"

I took a second to step outside and noticed that the ugly neon green that covered the entire outside of the dive club matched the trim color of a fancier looking club across the street. Was this really worth an argument? When I went back in they were finishing up their spat, and after a few more profanity-laden exchanges in which the other guy made some mentions of returning with a flamethrower, I was let in. The doorman was too focused on the flamethrower threat to bother taking my money and I wasn't going to push the issue.

The pair of gentlemen I was looking for were standing by the chicken wing buffet, debating the merits of chicken wings versus steak at a strip club. There was no way in hell I was going to touch anything in the club with my bare skin, let alone swallow it, but I needed to know where they were sitting so I had to hang out by the buffet with them and hold a plate and look like I was deciding between the red wings and the green wings while I eavesdropped. For a brief moment I wondered if the chef…"chef"…could make a sauce the exact color of the paint so they could send a batch across the street, but by the time I realized how weird it was that I was choosing sides in a strip club paint dispute my guys had disappeared.

I spent the next half hour looking for them. The place was surprisingly packed for such a crap hole, but the fog and mirrors and laser lights and fake boobs made it impossible so I finally left. But that's not the important part. Posey seemed happy with what I gave her information-wise (she had no opinion on the paint kerfuffle aside from my use of the word kerfuffle in her presence, which she thought was a lazy stylistic choice and would have preferred a word with more substance or a more detailed explanation of why I found the discussion worthy of mentioning at all) and didn't press me any harder about why I didn't have more information to offer. I went to sleep and dreamt of pulsating music and topless chicken wings. The next morning I'd been at work less than an hour when the same guys walked by my office.

At first I was excited, then I was pissed, then I was excited again, but then I was very depressed for getting excited in the wrong way. I wasn't excited about being able to help Posey; my first thought was that she had set me up and that this was going to be a good way for me to help Lindsey. My initial instinct was to call Lindsey, but I calmed myself down enough to pass on that bit of stupidity and decided to follow the guys instead. They were idiots, which should have made it easy, but I wasn't exactly a genius myself so we ended up evenly matched.

Each of them was fat in a different way. The taller of the two was fat like a football lineman. He was solid but big and wore sweat pants and a warm-up jacket. The shorter one was fat like a cliché. He was jiggly in all of the wrong places and wore baggy blue jeans scrunched up at the waist with a yellow bungee cord and a torn Batman T-shirt that hung just above his belly button. They wandered around the main hallway for several minutes, but didn't seem to be looking for anything or even waiting for anyone. I stood just inside my lab doorway so I could keep an eye on them without being seen. It was a slower day than even normal days so we were the only three people on the floor. When it looked like nothing was going to happen, I lost my patience and pushed the panic button.

"Can I help you guys?" I asked.

I expected them to scurry away, and wasn't really sure what I would do if they did—run after them maybe—but they didn't.

"Looking for the jizz rooms," Bungee Pants said.

His partner broke in to clarify before I could ask my awkward question.

"We're interested in making a deposit," Sweat Pants said.

"Uhhh..." I said. "Let me see if—"

"Do I know you?"

Shit. Was I going to blow it? What was there to blow?

"I'm going to go see if I can find—"

"He was at The Palace last night," Bungee Pants said. "Probably spying on us."

I wouldn't have pegged him as the astute one.

"I—"

"Guy likes titties and chicken wings. Don't make him a spy."

Oh god. Were they both astute? Was *I* the idiot?

"I was there about the paint," I said. "What a mess that is."

"Same fucking color," Bungee Pants said. "How does that even happen?"

"You mentioned you could find someone to help us," Sweat Pants said. "We're kind of in a hurry."

I nodded, flustered at my luck, and ran away. It took me fifteen minutes to track down someone who knew anything about the sperm lab and by the time I made it back with him, the pants brothers were gone. Had I been gone long enough for them to spy on me? Were they really interested in freezing their sperm? Would my internal narration continue sounding like a bad soap opera teaser?

• • •

LINDSEY FOUND me the next day at lunch and I told her about the brothers.

"They could be cousins for all I know," I said. "But for some reason I think they're brothers."

"And you think your wife put them onto you?"

"I don't know. Maybe? It just seems like a weird coincidence, you know?"

"And your boss doesn't know?"

"I didn't do anything."

"I need to talk to these guys," Lindsey said. "Maybe I can—"

"I got it. Trust me," I said.

I don't know that she trusted me, but she left me alone. I finished my lunch and went to meet a guy I knew in hospital security. His name was Ethan Hall and he was a computer genius and a nurse and a former combat pilot. We'd met during orientation and I was fascinated he could fly a helicopter and he was fascinated that I was a writer. He'd been begging me to use him as an expert source and this seemed as good a time as any.

I found him in his concrete bunker in the basement of the main hospital between the emergency room and the landing pad for the medical flight helicopter. It was always cold down there and it always smelled like jet fuel. I suspected those fumes had as much to do with him helping me as his helpful personality.

He already had the security video of my previous encounter with the brothers up on the screen and started running it for me.

"At first, yeah, it looks like they don't belong," Ethan said. "But digging back through the feeds you can see them both several other times looking right at home."

The video jumped to a string of shorter clips that showed the brothers individually doing a variety of what appeared to be janitorial and maintenance work.

"They're employees?" I asked.

He stopped the video and spun his chair toward me and handed me a sheaf of papers.

"Temporary, but yeah," he said.

The papers were printouts from the university staff directory and had pictured of the brothers, and it did seem they were brothers, at least from the last name. Oranthello and Lemon Carter lived over in East English Village, one of the few remaining stable and populated neighborhoods in the city.

"These are their real names?"

"Can't do nicknames or aliases in the HR system."

"Wow," I said.

"Nothing classified in there," he said. "So no trouble, but what you do with it…well—"

"I'll keep it to myself."

"These kinds of guys," he said. "I'm not perfect, I mean, I

shouldn't be showing you this, but—"

"They bring the whole place down," I said.

He nodded and slapped my shoulder. I wasn't sure how to take that and no easy out presented itself so I just left and went back to my desk. I ate the lunch Posey packed me while I thought about what to do next. I don't like to wait; I wanted to go out to their house and confront them. There was nothing keeping me at work and maybe I could even take Lindsey with me and wash my hands of the whole mess. Wait a few days for it to settle out, let Lindsey get what she needed, then give these guys to Posey so she could get what she needed. Then I'd be the good guy. What I needed.

And then what? Stay at the boring job. Build a boring life. Raise a boring kid. I could feel the pressure again. Torn between the stability and security of boring and the excitement of adventure, the lure of trouble. I was still a writer. I had a book deal. A book deal that called for me to write more books. I didn't want to write more books about boring guys with boring lives. I wanted to write about guys with names like Oranthello and Lemon.

I left my desk looking like someone was still working there in case anyone stopped by and then I drove out to East English Village feeling excited and nauseated. I actually turned around twice and tried to head back to the hospital, but ended up getting myself so lost it was closer to just go to the house. The address turned out to be on the outskirts of EEV in an area on the border of Detroit and Grosse Pointe that wasn't nearly as well maintained and populated as the media and community organizers would have you believe. I pulled off to the side of the road in front of a weedy lot a few houses down and waited to see if my nerve would show up. Instead, a tall black guy with a shotgun banged on my window and scared the hell out of me.

I wasn't sure if I was being carjacked or assaulted for being in the wrong neighborhood, but either way I was sure it was going to end with me dead. In the end, it wasn't my life that flashed before my eyes; it was disappointment that all of my worst racial prejudices had come true. After spending so much mental effort analyzing the social causes of poverty and crime and trying to understand the individuals separately rather than seeing them as just a race, I was going to be murdered by a black man for being white in the wrong neighborhood.

And then I wasn't. He was still outside my window and he still had his shotgun, but he was no longer facing me. He was turned looking behind us at a police cruiser that I recognized immediately as Lindsey. I wanted to fling my car door open and smack the guy with it, but I suspected it wouldn't go the way I saw it in my head and I'd just make it easier for him to turn back and shoot me. I also thought about driving away but I had no idea where I was and would likely end up on the wrong side of a dead-end street. So I sat there and waited to see how my fate would shake out.

My door opened anyway, because in my last remaining act of white guilt I had refused to lock my doors while driving through the neighborhood, and the big guy dragged me out of my car and into the street. But instead of murdering me he just drove away in my car and I laughed. I felt alive. I'd faced danger and hadn't died. Sure, I lost the car, but Posey had installed a GPS tracker on it and she'd send somebody out to find it. But I was still *alive*. And it was awesome. I was pretty sure I could never go back to a desk job again. I hopped to my feet and ran toward Lindsey's car, excited to share my epiphany with someone who could genuinely understand how equally awesome and fucked up that feeling was.

"You'll never believe what I'm feeling," I said as I opened the passenger door.

Well, tried to open the door. It was locked. I focused more on the inside of the car and saw that instead of Lindsey at the wheel there was a fat man in a tiny uniform.

He rolled down the window and said, "Stay the fuck away from my officers." Then drove away.

My cell phone was in my car because I didn't like how it dug into my leg when I drove, but even if I had it, there wasn't anyone I could call. Lindsey wasn't going to be any help apparently and there was no way in hell I was ready to explain to Posey what I was up to, so once again, I went all in on my plan, and knocked on the door I came to visit.

"Aw, fuck," the taller brother said. I couldn't remember from the sheets which one was which.

"Oranthello Carter," I said.

"Go away."

"I have an offer for you. For something you're already doing."

I could see him scanning the street in front of his house.

"Where's your car?"

"Guy with a shotgun took it just now."

He rubbed the top of his head and groaned.

"Fuck," he said. "Go away."

"I know about the sperm bank," I said. "What you're planning."

He closed the door on me so I knocked. A lot. There was no doorbell that I could see.

"My wife is your bail bondsman," I shouted at the door. "I can legally go ask your neighbors about you."

The door opened again and he pulled me inside and punched me in the stomach. I doubled over and crumpled to the ground with a bunch of wisecracks running through my head that I couldn't catch my breath long enough to spout off.

His brother had joined him by the time I got myself standing upright again so I prepared for a full-on beating. But they sat me down, offered me some sweet tea, and wanted to hear more about my plan.

"Toldja he was at the titty bar," Lemon said.

Oranthello grunted and handed me a cup of sun tea like my mom used to make.

"Punched you 'cause you come to my house and threatened me," he said.

"It's the only thing I could think of," I said.

"Doesn't mean we can't still find a way to do this."

"Oh, good. Okay then."

"Our terms," Lemon said. "We get free range to do our stuff and you don't say shit. Just keep—"

"We have some...complications," Oranthello said. "That you can help us with."

"With my wife?"

He shook his head.

"Got us confused with some other brothers she lookin' for with that."

"Oh," I said. Then it clicked. "*Oh.*"

"We're already on probation for some bullshit thing with a manager at the hospital who don't like us," Oranthello said.

"You want me to cover for you at work?"

He nodded. His brother was hopping around the couch drinking a tall boy from a generic white can.

"And you'll help me with what I need?"

He nodded again.

We drank some more tea and some more beer and plotted out our next move. They were short on details regarding their own plan, which was fine with me. The less I knew the less chance I had of being dragged into their mess. Or so it seemed at that moment. But in that moment I had a plan. I had a team and a notion of what was coming next. I'd come up with bullshit jobs for them to do in my lab and that would give them time to finish the last part of their own plan, which seemed to involve stealing a different sample. And while they were in there they'd get Titus's sample too. I still hadn't decided what to with it once I had it, but getting it was the hard part and these guys were going to make it a whole lot easier. The only remaining bit to negotiate was how I was going to get home.

"I need a ride," I said.

"Bus stop down the road about three blocks," Oranthello said.

"No way. I'm still a little freaked out from earlier."

"Boy got himself jacked out by the lot," Oranthello said to his brother. "Want a ride now."

"Give him the yellow car number. They got a special this month for—"

"I can't afford a taxi. You guys don't have a car?"

"I'd love to sit here and work this out and what it all means, but we got shit to do."

I really didn't have the money for a cab and there was no way I was ready to ask Posey for a ride so there was only one other person I could call for a help. The only number I had for him was his office at the university, so I hoped he was still sleeping there.

It took Parker Farmington almost an hour to pick me up and by the time he showed up Oranthello and Lemon had left for a memorial service for their cousin. When Parker was my thesis advisor I'd detested him and projected all of my own insecurities about my life and my writing onto him. His spot-on critiques of my work mixed with an abysmal teaching style honed through a decade of life in the emotional pressure cooker of academia made him an easy scapegoat for my failures. Recently, though, we'd built a fragile truce that had the potential for something approaching friendship. I offered him a glass of tea but he declined and seemed eager to leave. I couldn't blame him, but I had to stop for a second when I saw him head toward a minivan in front of the house.

"No way," I said. "Is that yours?"

"There are three cars in the driveway and nobody could

give you a ride?"

"None of them work. Why are you driving a minivan?"

"Just get in for god's sake and shut up."

I gave him space and quiet until we got out of the neighborhoods and closer to downtown. His driving was faster and more aggressive than it had been the last time we drove together even though the stakes were far lower. There were no signs in the van that he had been living in it, but I still suspected it. He'd had a rough time of life after our last adventure and he hadn't lucked into a wife and downtown loft like I had. We'd both had some success with our books, though, and had been signed to deals by the same publisher, who wanted us to cowrite a book with each of us telling the different sides of a crime gone wrong.

"Did you get the last round of pages I sent?"

"This business with Lindsey, you need to get it sorted out."

"You've got something going with her now?"

"It's not like that. It's not romantic. We've just been... talking. Sharing."

"Like sponsors?"

"It's hard to explain. But she's helped me work through a lot and she's still working through her own stuff."

We didn't speak again until he dropped me off in front of the Wade Bail Bonds office downtown across from the courthouse.

"I don't know where you live and I don't want to," he said.

"No, this is great. Thanks."

Awkward pause.

"Thanks for everything," I said. "I wouldn't mind talking sometime either."

Parker smiled and waved.

"Stop by my office tomorrow. We'll compare manuscripts and relive our last adventure."

• • •

A SUMMER cold that had been hanging around for too long was turning into the flu and I was starting to feel like crap so I found Posey's office whiskey stash and took a few shots of mid-level rye to push the bad thoughts out of my head. I wanted to spend the rest of the afternoon dreaming the fantasy of a big print book deal. It didn't take much of the whiskey and dreaming to put me to sleep and I woke a couple of hours later with a snotty headache and Posey standing over me with her phone held out toward my face.

"Explain this," she said.

"Uh, I guess we needed new phones because—"

"Look at the location," she said.

Ah, so it was time for that conversation. I should have planned what I was going to say better. I sat up and popped my back, trying to buy time for my brain to wake itself up as well.

"I got carjacked."

"Why didn't you tell me? Did you call the police?"

"Why would I call the cops?"

"I don't believe you."

"The cops wouldn't be any help and I figured—"

"About the car, not the cops."

"I was freaked out. I'm sorry."

"How did you get back here?"

"Parker drove me."

"Jesus. You called him before you called me? What are you

up to?"

"Nothing, I swear."

She put her phone down and sat on the desk next to me with her body language sagging into frustration.

"Come on, Dom. Tell me what's going on."

The best lies are based mostly in truth, right?

"I was trying to help," I said. "Those guys you gave me, they work at the university and this guy I know gave me their address."

"You went after them by yourself?"

"I just wanted to see what they were up to."

"And they stole your car?"

I gave her the rundown of what happened, omitting the part about Lindsey's boss and glossing over what we actually talked about. Her body language opened up and she seemed to relax more, but I knew she still didn't totally buy my story.

"You're an idiot, you know that, right?"

"I need to do something. You were right. I'm getting antsy at work and think there's something more out there for me."

She handed me a scrap of paper with an address on it.

"A guy I know has your car in his garage but you need to go get it."

"How am I supposed to get out there?"

"Take the bus, call a cab, I don't care. Just get out there before he closes at six."

"I heard Yellow Car is having a sale this month."

She handed me a wad of cash from the top drawer of her desk and picked her phone up from the floor and left without a word.

I was tempted to take the bus out to the garage to pick up my car because 1) I could keep the cash for frivolous spending Posey couldn't track with my debit card and 2) I'd heard it was a great source of dialogue and plot ideas for future books. I'd also heard horror stories of hours-long delays at the bus stop, and a surprising number of city buses had been hitting pedestrians lately. With the way I was feeling, I just wanted to get out there as quickly as possible and if I took a cab I could finish the nap Posey had so rudely interrupted. The nap was great, my car was retrieved without incident, and I felt so good about how the day was going I passed all of the cash I had left after paying the cabbie to the mechanic who saved the day.

It was quiet for three days before everything went to hell. Oranthello set things in motion just after lunch time on a Monday. I'd called off work because my flu had reached apocalyptic levels and I'd spent my small reserve of energy staying awake for *Let's Make a Deal* and *The Price Is Right*. I hated the afternoon news and after that it's nothing but soap operas and paternity test shows so I'd fallen into a deep NyQuil slumber and was ill-equipped to deal with what I was about to hear.

"We have a problem," Oranthello said.

"I'm really not…I'm kinda sick today so can we—"

"I got what you wanted, but—"

That woke me up a bit more. I sat up on the couch and tried to pay closer attention to what he was saying.

"You have the sample? Wow. Great. We need to get it quick before—"

"There's been a *problem,*" he said again.

He went on to explain that they'd been surprised during their heist and his brother had been shot and they'd only been able to grab one sample instead of two.

"But you got the one I needed. That's what matters."

"Yours is the cheap one, man. We had to leave the money one behind."

"So what do you want? You want money?"

"A hundred thousand dollars. By tomorrow."

"No way. I can't get that."

"You tipped us off then you called in sick so we could get set up. I want my fucking money."

He hung up before I could continue arguing, but the threat was implicit. Get the money or go to jail for robbery and possibly murder if Lemon died. I ran to the bathroom and threw up violently before passing out next to the toilet.

Posey called me next, while I was out, and left a voicemail that just said, "What happened?"

Finally I heard from Lindsey, who showed up at the door

with a blood-splattered uniform and a gun pointed at me.

"One chance," she said. "Tell me what you did."

"I've got the flu. I didn't do anything. I don't know—"

She fired twice into the living room and hit the TV and the ceiling.

"I swear to god," I said. "I don't know what's going on."

She came inside the house and closed the door behind her, but kept her gun pointed at me.

"I got a call that somebody was breaking into the freezer and when I showed up your friends were stealing my sample. Tell me why."

She shook her gun hand at me and I backed away from her.

"They were supposed to be helping me, helping *us*. But I was out sick today."

"You look like shit."

"Now they want a hundred grand to give the sample back."

I don't know why I said it. I needed to say something and that was the first thing that popped out. My brain was still mushy and I hadn't been in control of it for the better part of the day.

"Fuck."

"Did you shoot Lemon?"

"Where's your wife?"

"I don't know anything. Put the gun down."

She did and I let out a huge breath.

"We need to get out of here," I said. "I'm sure somebody heard your stupid shots and called the police and I can't be here until I figure out what's going on."

It didn't take much to convince her that she didn't want to be there when they showed up either so I took her out the back way through the tenants' exit into the garage. The loft had been used by Titus as a safe house and was ridiculously secure while he lived in a dump of a house on the west side of the city that had been in their family for years. Posey decided she wanted to live in the loft and sold the house for $1,000 and a new iPad to a group of Russian investors.

My car was where I'd left it the other day and I tossed the keys to Lindsey.

"Cops are better drivers than writers," I said. "Get us someplace safe."

Before she pulled away though, I stopped her and got out of the car. I popped the small GPS unit off the underside of the back bumper and stuck it to the wall of my parking space then checked my phone to make sure location services were turned off. I felt horrible doing it and couldn't have felt more like I was cheating than if I got in the car with a condom and chocolates for Lindsey, but it felt like the right thing to do to isolate my exposure to people who could complicate things.

"I'm really not sure where to go," Lindsey said. "I don't have a safe room or secret club house or anything."

"We're not hiding," I said. "We need to find those two boneheads."

I gave her the address of the brothers' house and described where it was.

"I know where it is," she said softly.

"Your boss showed up the last time I was there and told me to stay away from you."

She snapped her head toward me without slowing down.

"Nobody gets it. This is my life. My legacy. I could die after this and sure, they'd talk about what I did…what I've done…"

Swerve out of traffic and a hard correction to the left to avoid a ditch.

"But a kid, my kid, with Titus, that's what was meant to be. That kid can..."

She looked back to the road and wiped her eyes with her sleeve. I thought about the kid I had on the way; I also thought about the kid I lost and what my legacy would be. For the longest time I pinned my legacy to my writing. But I looked at Lindsey and thought about her history and Titus Wade's history and the idea that the offspring of two awful people could become a positive legacy.

"And you put me in a position to screw up *my* kid and *my* legacy," I said. "I shouldn't be in the middle of this. Your legacy shouldn't come at the cost of mine."

Lindsey parked my car in the driveway behind a rusted out Grand Prix with two spare tires on the left side and the trunk tied down with a rope. She still had her gun with her but it was down to just two shots. She also had a Taser, but it was only good at close range and I suspected if things were going to go to shit here they were going to go to shit at a distance.

"I've got a riot gun in here," I said, popping the trunk. "Last I checked it had rubber loads so I don't kill anyone by mistake."

"You know they're not here, right?" Lindsey said when we were almost to the house. "They'd have to be stupid to be here."

"We've both seen knuckleheads like this jump bail or escape prison or whatever and the first place they go is back to their momma's house."

"Still. Seems like a stretch."

"I don't expect to find them in there with your sperm sample waiting to shoot us up when we approach, no. But maybe their locks are shit or maybe their neighbor is a cousin or a friend who knows where they are."

"Then maybe I shouldn't be wearing my uniform."

"You can stay in the house or the car and I'll go knocking."

"With a shotgun? Out here, all pasty white? Won't need to worry about what you'll say to your wife 'cause you won't see her again."

We didn't even make it up the driveway before a neighbor proved her right.

"Hell you doing out this way?" an old black man in long sleeves and a blood red fez who was holding his own shotgun hollered at us.

"Not gonna lie and say I'm a friend," I said. "The guys who live here took something from me and I want it back."

"That why you brought a cop?"

I looked back at Lindsey. She looked like a mess and not like a typical cop.

"Campus security, not a cop."

"You two go in there all bent and start shooting one of those bullets gonna hit me or my dog or one of the kids sleeping on a couch up and down this block."

"Riot load," I said, holding the gun up. "Wife won't let me use real bullets so she gives me bean bags. Kind of a profound metaphor for my life, isn't it?"

"Instead of shouting across the yard for everyone to hear, maybe we can go inside and quiet the hell down," Lindsey said.

"I'm just trying to do the right thing," he said, letting the gun hang to his side.

"Do you know where these guys are?" Lindsey asked.

"Don't see 'em hangin' round with nobody round here," he

said.

"They mentioned a cousin the other day," I said. "Some kind of memorial service. Anybody like that live around here?"

"Cousins, sure. Everybody got cousins round here."

He pointed with his gun down round the way we'd come.

"End of the block there is an auntie they got named Hetta. Seems stupid enough to take 'em in after whatever they done."

We gave him our thanks for the help and for not shooting us and got the hell out of there. A few steps toward our destination I noticed a suspicious van coming toward us. Again, I felt bad for thinking the car was suspicious because it was too nice and it was running. Had they seen us at the house? Were they going to the house? Were they involved in the robbery? I nudged Lindsey with my elbow, but she ignored me and looked ahead and not at the van as it passed us. I couldn't help but turn around to see if the van pulled into the driveway, but instead, the van turned the corner and disappeared.

"Weird," I said.

"Keep walking," Lindsey said.

"What's with the voice. You're freaking—"

"*Keep* walking."

The tone chilled me so I kept walking. We didn't go to the aunt's house, we walked back to the car where Lindsey took the wheel and drove us away as quickly as possible.

"What the hell was that?" I asked when the time was right.

"I know that van."

"More cops?"

"Prison guards," she said. "I don't know for sure but the pieces are there and—"

"Why would prison guards be out here looking for two

hooligans?"

"I went with Titus to some of his treatments," she said. "He didn't want anyone to know, especially…well, you know who. And—"

"I thought he hated you."

"Every time we went, I saw a van like that out front and there was this guy who was supposed to be a big deal gangster getting cancer treatments."

I knew what she was talking about and had seen the same thing. The prisons in Michigan didn't have radiation treatment equipment at their facilities so if an inmate needed treatment they were brought to a state hospital in leg irons with armed escorts. If Lindsey knew this guy and they were sniffing around the brothers' house, I had an idea what that meant too.

"Oh shit," I said by way of acknowledgment.

"We don't know yet. We can't panic," she said. "But it makes sense."

They were going to kidnap the sperm sample of a gangster under cancer treatment when they took Titus's sample instead for me.

"The money sample," I said out loud.

"The what?"

"Oranthello Carter called me after they left the lab and said he could only take one sample and that was ours. He said he left the money sample behind."

"That doesn't make any sense. Why not take the money sample and forget ours?"

"Wouldn't explain the gangster's guards scouting out their house either."

"Shit," she said, smacking her hand on the steering wheel

while she was still driving. "Shit shit *shit*."

"Posey has a file on these guys. We need to bring her in."

"Fuck," she said. "Fuck fuck fuck fuck fuck."

"We need to get their bail file. It'll have addresses, next of kin, phone numbers, the sort of stuff that makes it easier to find guys who don't want to be found."

She groaned and screamed something that sounded like my name mixed with a curse word and then pulled off to the side of the road.

"I think I fucked my head up," she said. "You need to drive."

I want to think what happened next was because of the cold medicine or because I was distracted or because Lindsey was a superior predator. But the minute she hit me with the Taser I knew it was just because I was an idiot.

I regained consciousness in the trunk of what I assumed was my car. Physically, I was fine and Lindsey hadn't bothered to tie my hands or legs or anything. But mentally I was melting down. This was going as bad as it possibly could go and, once again, it was my fault. I'd been suffering from PTSD from the last time one of my stupid ideas backfired and ended up with me knocked out in my own damn car, but this was worse. I was in the trunk and more was at stake than my literary pride or the dreams of a nut job serial killer.

The darkness of the trunk was a theater for the horrible memories socked away in my brain. I kept flashing back to seeing Titus shot in the head and then seeing Posey kneeling next to his body before we ground it to a mash. I missed my wife. I missed my kid that hadn't even been born yet and I was paralyzed with a burning pain running the length of my arms and legs. I wanted to die and wanted to live. I wanted to haunt the fuck out of Lindsey and I wanted to be Posey's guardian angel.

Fuck. Deep breath. It's a trunk, not a coffin.

Still burning. Deep breath.

More burning but lower. Calmer. Slower breath.

Shit. No. Ahhhhhh.

Little-known cure for PTSD and claustrophobia: peeing your pants.

The warmth went from relaxing to cold and itchy though. It wasn't long before I couldn't breathe again. The smell was awful. I was embarrassed. I needed to get the pants off. It was the first pair of Old Navy jeans I'd ever owned and they turned out to be surprisingly easy to remove in the trunk of a car. They were soft and slid easily off once I had them unbuttoned. I was determined to write the best letter ever to the Old Navy company one day and explain how the ease of getting out of their jeans may have saved my life. Maybe I'd write it as a short story. Maybe an essay. Shit, why had I never considered writing a memoir before?

My shoes proved harder to remove than my jeans though. Despite how painful they were on my feet, I still wore the same pair of Converse All-Star low tops I'd been wearing since I started grad school. They were the only thing that still identified me as a writer and I didn't want to ruin them. But they weren't coming off and I couldn't reach the laces in my current position.

I know what you're thinking. The trunk was going to open and I was going to be in my underwear. Haha. Stupid writer.

Wrong. The underwear came off even easier than the jeans. I was hoping whoever opened the trunk would be so shocked to see a naked dude that it would buy me a few seconds to kick or run or...wait a second. She wouldn't be that stupid, would she?

I felt around next to me and behind me and through the entire small range of motion I had in the trunk but couldn't find the riot gun. Well, I guess that would have been too convenient for my current plot line (I knew my verve for writing was coming back when I started envisioning my life as a running story line in which I was the main character).

Wait. No. This was even worse. My last grab was down into the space by the spare tire that was digging into my spleen and instead of the riot gun I came up with Lindsey's small revolver in my hand. Now I had a choice. I could certainly point the gun and pretend I would shoot whoever was in the sightline when they opened the trunk, but I knew that would never happen. I was already haunted by the vision of a bullet going through Titus Wade's head, there was no way I could recover from—

"What the hell?"

I fired once and then, not wanting to wait to see if she was going to help me or strangle me, I rolled out of the trunk and started running. Rather, I started hobbling because my shoes were still on and my pants and underwear were around my ankles and I couldn't move very quickly. It wasn't long before I fell over and scraped my knees. On the way down, I caught a glimpse of Lindsey on the ground by my car grabbing her leg. Shit, had I actually hit her? There was really no time to stick around and find out. I pulled up my pants and underwear, itchy cold and all, and ran back to my car and drove away. There wasn't a second of guilt on my part for leaving her there shot with her own gun and I was ready to reconnect with my wife and beg her forgiveness (and protection).

But I couldn't find her. She didn't answer her phone or the

office phone and she wasn't at the apartment or the office. I stayed at the office to contemplate the meaning of all of this and didn't like where it led. Sure, she liked to work on her own and wasn't keen on checking in with me all of the time, but she always answered her phone. She was one of the few people I knew who still preferred phone calls to text messages because she liked to read the emotion from the caller. It gave her power a text message would never approach. I sent a text message just to be sure and had an idea. If my car and my phone could be tracked, I wondered what the chances were that Posey's phone and car were on GPS as well.

I had little faith that her phone had any tracking features on it that she wouldn't have already disabled, but I was pretty sure her car would still be live. It took me a few minutes to remember how to log into the tracking web site, but I was able to find the email she sent me with instructions and had it pulled up quickly after that. The map on the website was always glitchy when Posey tried to load the coordinates into her own phone so I was transferring it over to Google Maps when the address triggered the imaginary light bulb over my head.

When the address was plugged in, I switched it to street view so I could get a good look at the house. When I saw that Posey's car was at the house she had allegedly sold to an investor I knew she was a more active participant in this mess than I expected. Somehow that made me feel better than if she had been on the outside looking in with it.

I felt good, but unsure how to proceed. I felt betrayed, which sucked and double sucked because of the irony of my own betrayal of her, but I also felt overwhelmed. As many stupid mistakes as I'd made the last time I got caught up in murder and heists, I always had a very clearly defined (if insane) goal. I didn't have that this time and that made it hard to focus my action. Getting to Posey seemed like a good first step, but if she was already onto something I wasn't sure if me charging in there would ruin whatever she was working on. I couldn't go to the police and I sure as hell couldn't go to Lindsey, so once again, I was left with Parker Farmington as my last resort for help. Maybe in his secret sponsor conversations he'd had with Lindsey he'd picked up on something that could help me.

• • •

I FOUND Parker at the recently opened Whole Foods near the university campus. It had become his de facto office since returning to the university after a brief sabbatical to deal with everything we'd been through. It was one of the few reminders left that when I first met him he had been a pretentious crunchy hippie wearing locally sourced clothes and driving a hybrid car. He'd since been broken down to a guy like me who favored greasy dives, thrift store clothes, and staying home all the time. But the Whole Foods was the only place in the entire Midtown area with easy parking so organic coffee and sustainable free Wi-Fi would have to do.

The few times we'd met since Titus Wade's impromptu wake at an industrial grinding shop in Toledo he told me he had trouble facing down the other faculty members and spent as little time on campus as possible. He, like myself, spent most of his time pretending to write, though he spent more time procrastinating through research where I spent my time procrastinating through publishing industry research.

"You realize how awkward this is," Parker said, pouring half of the tiny bottle of bourbon I brought him into his coffee.

"Lindsey?"

He nodded. Big slurp of bourbon coffee.

"Love?"

"A bit, sure. Lot of lust, some guilt, and convenience as well."

"You know about the pact with God, right?"

"Enough of it."

"Got us a couple fucked up women, eh?"

He finished the coffee and stared at his plate. Some sort of breakfast burrito concoction that spilled over the edges of his already ample dish.

"Why are you here?"

I ran my fingers over the table top made from a recycled car trunk and had a flashback to last Christmas when I stood at the edge of a storage facility and watched Titus Wade Taser Parker and shove him into the trunk of his car at my request. Eventually I stole the car back from Titus and let Parker out. After a gunfight with assassins in the bathroom of a Niagara Falls honeymoon suite, the long drive back to Detroit, and the shared experience of surviving a ridiculous amount of surreal life-or-death experiences, we reconciled our differences enough to return to the university as guarded acquaintances rather than enemies.

I gave him a brief rundown of everything that had happened so far. He didn't laugh when I mentioned running down the street with my pants around my ankles. I suspected on some level he still hated me for what I had done to him and what I had wanted to do to him.

"I should have probably gone back for her," I said.

"When she's fixed she'll come to you."

"I figured as much," I said. "You want me to drive so you can finish your booze coffee?"

"No more booze, no more coffee," he said. "I'll drive."

I was happy to see Lindsey wasn't dead in the street when we pulled up to her house. She lived in Midtown near the university campus in a nice strip of duplex condos that was bordered by the student ghetto on one side and an actual, burned out ghetto on the other. I couldn't help but laugh at how on-the-nose the visual was for Midtown's split personality these days.

The student ghetto, where I'd spent most of my time during graduate school, was mostly made up of rich kids from the suburbs paying sky high rents for dilapidated apartments so they could feel edgy and urban, watching the poor people and the downtrodden like zoo animals. While across the street people lived in shells of houses that had been built by hand by their grandparents or great-grandparents and they were too stubborn, too prideful, or too poor to move anywhere else even as arson remained Detroit's favorite pastime. When the college kids graduated their student ghetto would be torn down and replaced by more upscale condos, which would eventually be torn down to make way for a sports stadium loaded with luxury boxes and gourmet food windows. And those in the burned out ghetto would plant flowers in ashes, paint murals on abandoned houses, mow their patchy lawns, and hope their kids would get lucky and get away.

Parker went to the door first and knocked while I waited in the driveway. When the garage door began opening, I stepped back toward the car and looked for possible escape routes. Lindsey was standing in the garage pointing the riot gun at me.

"Ooh la la," I said.

"Bean bag to the head kills as much as a bullet."

"You put me in my own goddamn trunk," I said. "It freaked me out. I've been having...you know, I mean what happened over Christmas was—"

"You need to talk to somebody about that."

"Like Parker?"

"He understands," she said, poking me in the chest with the barrel of the riot gun. "*You* need to understand."

"I don't know what to do. We need to fix this."

Parker had stayed on the porch while I chatted up Lindsey, but he was now next to me breathing heavily.

"Why don't we go inside for some privacy," he said.

"You bothered about maybe being seen outside with a beefy woman with a gun and giant boobs?"

"I wouldn't call them giant," he said. "But you two aren't very welcome in this part of town and I'm not comfortable with anyone driving by and reporting me with you."

"Fine, come on in, grandpa."

I was excited to get into Lindsey's house. Curiosity and research are great excuses for writers to be nosy and I was the nosiest of the bunch. Being able to satisfy any curiosity I could think of was the only good part of the brief time I spent as a newspaper reporter. And as big a role as Lindsey had played in my last mess, the most personal place I'd spent any significant time with her was her patrol car. And her condo looked like the inside of a patrol car.

It was utilitarian to a ridiculous degree and smelled vaguely of vomit and urine. Her furniture looked like it had been picked up at garage sales and swap meets, but wasn't dirty or gross. The main floor was only a living room in the front with a kitchen, small dining room, and bathroom in the back. The kitchen was more like a bar, with a series of liquor bottles filling the counters where others had spices and cookie jars. The stove was clean in the way only a stove that was never used could be clean. The microwave, on the other hand, looked like a decade of frozen dinners had taken root inside.

Lindsey caught me looking around and said, "Stop looking for secrets. I'm barely ever here."

"Maybe we should go into the basement," I said, nodding toward the stairs off to the side of the kitchen by a back door leading to a small patio. "So nobody sees us through the windows or anything."

"You're not snooping through my basement," she said. "Sit down. Have a drink. I think I have some cereal that hasn't gone bad."

"Our mutual friend here thinks he knows where the crooks are," Parker said.

"Mutual friend? I don't know about that," Lindsey said.

"I tracked Posey's car. She's at..."

I looked over at Parker and then at Lindsey and couldn't bring myself to say it.

"No way," Lindsey said. "She didn't."

"She kept her brother's house, yes. And didn't tell him," Parker said.

"And she's there now?"

I nodded.

"Then let's go get her file on these guys while she's gone."

"I think we need more thought and evaluation," Parker said. "Before we do anything silly."

"Like shove somebody in a trunk?"

"Or pop 'em in the leg with their own gun?"

"I freaked out," I yelled. "What did you expect? What the hell were you going to do with me?"

"We don't need your stupid wife tagging along. We need her stupid file."

I looked at Parker for his thoughts.

"You said it yourself," he said. "You can't trust her."

"Do we know for sure they have what *you* need?"

"Why would they lie about it? If we get them the money and they don't have the sample they know we'll come after them."

Lindsey flopped into a plastic chair between her kitchen table and the refrigerator and reached for the closest liquor bottle. It looked at casual glance to be a vodka bottle.

"There's some Kool-Aid in the fridge," she said to me. "Can you pour me a glass if it's not too much trouble?"

"Kool-Aid? Are you twelve? I eat like a toddler and I don't even drink Kool-Aid," I said.

"We're talking, not drinking," Parker said. "We need to establish for sure they have the sample Lindsey wants. How do we do that?"

Lindsey unscrewed the cap from the vodka bottle and was in the middle of taking a swig when Parker smacked the bottle out of her hand. The bottle exploded against the counter and sent glass and liquor flying through the entire kitchen.

"Jesus. What the hell?" Lindsey screamed.

"Drunk or not," I said, "none of us are any good without our eyes."

Parker pulled Lindsey to her feet and away from the table.

"This is your bullshit," he told her. "I want to help you because you've helped me, and you've helped Dominick. He's certainly made the situation worse with another one of his stupid plans. But if we all learned anything from the last time it's that involving more people and more weapons will not turn out well. We need to contain this, and evaluate this, and make a plan. Now go change your clothes and clear your head."

She did it and I wasn't surprised. As much as I had despised Parker Farmington as a professor, the reason he'd been my thesis advisor was because I craved his validation. He was smart and savvy and had a way of convincing people to trust him even as he belittled them. I hesitated to liken it to an abusive relationship, but a lot of the brain wiring had to be the same. His greatest skill was spotting someone's weakness and pushing them until they cracked or changed.

My vanity and awareness of my own weaknesses had been ripe for him, but it wasn't until we'd been pushed to the edge of our survival together that I realized in his own sadistic and awkward way he was trying to help me. I could see the roots of the same kind of help brewing in what he had with Lindsey. I just hoped we all lived long enough to revel in the success and epiphanies.

"Find a broom and clean this up," Parker said.

I chose to believe it was because he knew tedious cleaning helped calm me when I got overwhelmed rather than that he was just being a dick.

I did a lousy job of cleaning up the broken glass while Parker and Lindsey did a lousy job of pretending they didn't care. But we had a plan, sort of, and knew what our next move was going to be. That seemed like progress.

In her mess of Titus things, a mess I was happy not to have seen despite my rampant curiosity, Lindsey found a sheet that had the registration number of Titus Wade's sample. We were off to find one of the surprisingly robust number of pay phones in the city of Detroit, which said more about the depressing state of life for residents of the city than it did about the longevity of the pay phone. I had the number Oranthello called me from saved in my phone and a list of pay phones Posey used to call around on bail jumpers when she didn't want to be traced.

We found the phone we were looking for at a church about a mile from Posey's house near the Motor City Casino. The phone was at the end of the parking lot away from the church and near the Goodwill donation bin. This made it a perfect spot to call from while providing a good view of the surrounding area in case anyone was following us. Oranthello answered the phone after the first ring and he still sounded pissed.

"If you want this money," I said, "prove you have our sample."

"You want me to put it on the phone to say hello?"

"Find the registration number," I said.

"It's on the bottom," Lindsey shouted.

"Fuck this shit," he said. "I ain't readin' no numbers to you. I want my money or I'll flush this shit down the toilet."

"Motherfucker," Lindsey shouted. "Prove it or I'll burn your house down."

"She seems serious," I said.

"Goddammit. Give me a number to call you at."

"I'll call you back in ten minutes," I said. "It shouldn't take you any longer than that."

I hung up convinced he was lying. I breathed a sigh of relief that they couldn't do shit to either of us and they were just swatting at flies until they caught a slow one. Ten minutes later, from a pay phone outside of a Mexican social club surrounded by live chickens, I called him back and he gave me the numbers exactly.

"Tomorrow," he said. "Or I flush it."

"They could have written the number down before," I said. "Why didn't he have it nearby?"

"They have to keep it frozen," Parker said. "Maybe they're not by the freezer."

"I know where there's a freezer that's perfect for this," I said, then I pointed to Lindsey. "And you do too."

"He always said it was big enough to fit a body in if he ever had to."

"Lots of room for whatever weird ice they need for these things."

"Taking him at his word on this one," Parker said. "Still doesn't mean it's the *only* one he has."

Shit. He was right. The schemer side of my brain was always a failure of imagination.

"They squeeze both of us, say they only had time to take just one, which raises the value of it substantially."

"Parker can check the lab," Lindsey said. "We're doing all this James Bond bullshit running from phone to phone for these yokels, but nobody's looking for *him*."

Parker sighed. I recognized it immediately as his pandering sigh. I'd heard it plenty in my workshops.

"It wasn't just because the two of you are connected to this that we can't go into the lab," he said. "It's a crime scene. No one can go into that lab."

"No," I said, feeling an odd emotion that felt vaguely like leadership bubble up, "we assume it's a crime scene. We *assume* no one can go in there. But we don't know."

I looked directly at Parker, expecting another sigh, but he nodded approval instead.

"We need to know," he said.

Despite my false bravado, I was decidedly mixed in my emotions about going back. It was easier to pretend things were being blown out of proportion and that everything would eventually work out if I didn't see anything in person. But I was sick of dodging life and being a casual observer. I'm a slow learner but one of the few lessons that had managed to stick with me from my last mess was that the way I was previously living my life was destined for failure. I hadn't yet figured out what would lead to success, but dodging this seemed too much like reverting to previous behavior and I didn't want that.

"What the hell was that?" Lindsey asked.

"He was narrating his thoughts out loud," Parker said.

I shrugged; by this point my eccentricities didn't surprise either of them. My guess is they were shocked I managed to function without drooling and running into walls every day and I was happy to cultivate that impression and hoped to take advantage of it at some point.

We drove to the hospital in silence and, in my case, nausea, as Parker didn't believe in air conditioning in his beat up old foreign car. The Detroit State University Medical Center is a collection of five hospitals of varying repute a few blocks over from the university campus. On the outside of the giant H that made up the complex were the world-renowned children's hospital and cancer center at one end while the VA hospital and specialty hospital that made most of its money from affiliated suburban surgery centers anchored the other end. I worked at the shitty receiving hospital in the middle of the H that represented everything wrong with the modern American health care system.

Lindsey directed Parker around to a circle drive at the back of the complex by the Simon Specialty Hospital. The labs were part of the medical school facility that made up most of the Simon's tenants and the cancer center rented space from them for their patients. The plan was to send Parker in as a scout to see what state the lab was in at the moment and we'd figure out the rest of our plan based on what he came back with. It didn't take long for him to come back with bad news.

"They have it locked down tight," he said. "I think we're screwed."

"I have one more idea," I said. "I know a guy who might be able to help."

Parking is a mess around the hospital and campus security disturbingly ambitious about ticketing violators, so someone had to stay with the car. I was the one who knew where we were going and I thought Lindsey's presence as an officer of the law would compromise any sketchy edge I might be able to get with my friend, so she sat in the car while Parker came with me. I would have preferred to go alone, but this was the least objectionable of the possible pairings, which was not a conclusion I'd ever expected to come to. As we wound our way through the bowels of the hospital, I gave Parker a rundown of how I knew the guy we were going to see and how he had helped me track down the home address of the Carter brothers.

"I was really hoping you'd learned your lesson," Parker said.

We were in a gross hallway connecting the specialty hospital to the receiving hospital that was as much a dividing line between the haves and the have-nots in the city as the mythical Eight Mile Road divide. With an extra special odor of urine and cold sewage. I wanted to stop and do a dramatic turn around to face Parker and have him clarify what in the hell he was talking about, but the smell really was awful and I wanted to get above ground as quickly as possible. At the end of the hallway we could have taken the elevator, which would have been quicker but had a nasty reputation for getting stuck. So we took the steps. I took them two at a time and was standing all dramatic-like at the door when Parker emerged.

"What's that supposed to mean?" I asked.

"I can't do this again," he said. "This shit. This is shit."

"Hanging out with me?"

"This caper shit. We're not cut out for it. We're not criminals."

He wasn't saying anything I hadn't thought a hundred times over, but I couldn't let him know we shared an opinion.

"I'm helping a friend," I said. "Nothing more."

"I read your new book, what you turned in of it before you fell into whatever stupor you've been in lately."

I knew he was playing me. I knew he had an angle. But I fell for it anyway.

"Really?"

"You're making progress in your writing that doesn't seem to be translating into your real life."

I let out an exasperated sigh and threw my arms in the air.

"What am I supposed to do? I want the boring stable life; I want to be responsible and take care of my family. But my wife is insane and frankly so am I. I can't handle responsibility and my writing suffers when I'm too comfortable."

"I see a future with Lindsey," he said.

"What's that have to do with—"

"I don't see it ending well. But I want to see it through anyway. I need to *know* how it ends."

"So you can write about it?"

"Maybe. I just need to know."

"Oh. So you're fucked up too."

"But I can't do this. We can't do this."

"There's still a chance," I said, regulating my words as carefully as I could, "that my guy tells us there's nothing to worry about. This could still all be a ruse."

He shrugged pathetically and shuffled fully out of the stairwell.

"Doesn't matter," he said. "It's not going to end well."

• • •

PARKER STAYED in the hallway pacing like a nervous kid outside the principal's office while I talked to Ethan Hall for the second time in as many weeks. He was twitchier this time and less enthusiastic about helping me, but I was still able to get some useful info out of him.

"Security taped it off," he said. "I don't think the police have even been here."

"So it's not a crime scene?"

He shook his head.

"Hazmat, I think. Workers comp maybe."

"But no cops?"

"The corrections guys were poking around in there too."

"The money sample," I said.

"The what?"

"Never mind. Just babbling to myself."

I thanked him and grabbed Parker by the shoulder. I told him what I'd learned and told him we were going to go into the lab and everything was going to be fine.

"Oh, I don't think that's likely at all," he said.

"You've always had a nasty pessimistic streak," I said, leading him back through the intestines of the complex and its stink, "but this fatalism is new. Is that from the other stuff?"

"You call kidnapping me and almost murdering me *stuff*?"

"That's not a conversation we're going to keep having," I

said. "You want to nurse a grudge go do it somewhere else. I thought we were moving on."

"I thought a lot of things a while ago, I try not to think much now if I don't have to."

I stopped and turned to look at him. This was getting weird even for him. His movements had slowed to almost nothing and his face was starting to lose its shape like his skull was melting.

"Dude, you okay?"

"Imagonnabe…ohshitIdiditbadthistime…"

And then he passed out right in a puddle of sewage water. I'm embarrassed to admit how close I came to leaving him there and running back to Lindsey, but he made some valid points about things I'd done to him, and no matter how skewered my good intentions had been, I still owed him almost as much as I owed Lindsey and this seemed like a good way to help even the score. I made my way back to Ethan's video dungeon and had him call for help.

The paramedics showed up quickly and swept him away, leaving me to stare awkwardly at Ethan and try to explain what had happened and what kind of mess I was in. I needed allies I didn't owe horrible favors to and he seemed like a good place to start. When I was done he had a great idea.

"You can use a disguise," he said. "There are masks all over this place."

I needed to get back up to Lindsey and let her know what was going on, but that also would mean bringing her into this in a more active role. Though in the short time I'd known her, she had proven to be impatient enough that it wouldn't surprise me to find out she'd left the car and was already looking for me.

"Jesus Christ," Lindsey said, "are you taking a leak down

here or looking for my stuff?"

"Who are you?" Ethan asked. "Who is she?"

"Where's Parker?"

"He passed out," I said. "It was really weird and so we called the paramedics and they—"

"Shit," she said. "Goddammit."

"I'm going to go back to the lab though, in disguise," I said.

"Oh."

Her change in demeanor gave me a clear indication of what Parker was talking about when he said any kind of relationship with Lindsey would end badly. I'd just mentioned that he had passed out in a puddle of sewer water but all she was concerned with was the possibility she might be able to get back the sperm sample from her dead ex-lover. I felt bad for Parker, but it also brought back all of the ways this thing could go wrong for my relationship as well. I squashed those to the back of my mind, though, and just hoped I'd be able to find a way to work it all out along the way.

"I'm thinking hazmat crew," Ethan said. "The suits are all over the place and people generally don't bother anyone wearing one."

"Who are you again?" Lindsey asked.

I introduced them and she nodded along. Unsure of how the various campus security factions got along with each other, I was nervous about a turf war, but Ethan seemed excited to keep helping so we went to find some hazmat suits lying around.

The recent Ebola scares had rained down a treasure trove of identity-concealing containment suits and the quick dissolution of the scare left them abandoned almost everywhere around the hospital. We found ours in the student nursing locker room.

Ethan was right about no one coming near us dressed in the suits. The few times we encountered people on the way to the lab they scattered quickly. We were in the hallway right outside the door to where I'd been sitting discussing how to approach our entry, when three uniformed officers emerged from under the caution tape. I had no way of knowing if the two in gray fatigues were the corrections officers Lindsey and I had seen outside the Carter brothers' house, so I ran.

I was back at the circle drive before I checked to see if Lindsey and Ethan had followed me. They hadn't because they hadn't panicked and they'd remembered that their identities were hidden behind the suits. I was roasting in my suit and the door I had gone in was locked and I couldn't muster the effort to take off my suit, walk all the way around to the side entrance, put the suit back on, and head back to the lab. And even if I did have the energy, I didn't imagine it would take Lindsey and Ethan long to see if the sample we wanted was in the lab so I took my suit off and sat in the backseat of the car with the windows down and enjoyed a moment of breezy calm.

I must have dozed off because I felt like I'd been underwater when I opened my eyes to the vaguely familiar sound of Lindsey's voice. Once I shook off the nap haze, she and Ethan were in the car and we were driving away.

"We should check on Parker," I said when Lindsey joined me outside the car. "I think something is—"

"You're a pussy," Lindsey said. "And a shitty friend and I hope you and your wife rot to death of boredom in that fucking apartment."

It was hard to hear but made me realize I was doing the smart thing by tapping out. I felt a wave of relief rush over me as I made my way up to Posey's office, where I was surprised to find her sitting behind her desk. It was one more sign that I had been too inside my head to see right from wrong and I chided myself for thinking Posey was petty enough to work something like this behind my back and hang me out to dry. I smiled when she caught my glance and was running through whether to eat or do some writing when she threw a stapler at me.

"What are you helping her do?" she asked.

"Absolutely nothing."

It felt good to say that and mean it.

"You were at the lab with her. You've been around town with her. You're doing something with her and it makes me wonder why you'd lie—"

"I told her I'm out. She's getting crazy. I can't be part of—"

"You don't get it, Dominick. This isn't about you. You keep trying to cram this shit into that weird little book brain of yours and match everything up to a story. But you're not a hero. I'm not a love interest and that crazy friend of yours isn't your sidekick."

I smiled at the thought of Lindsey being my sidekick instead of the other way around, but all that did was enrage Posey more. Despite her comment, I really was trying to see this outside of my world and that's why I was having trouble understanding what all the fuss was about. I had no siblings so I couldn't relate to the manic passion Posey had about maintaining her brother's estate and seeing to his final wishes, and I had never loved anyone in the sort of tragic, violent manner that Lindsey did so her pursuit of a child with a dead man baffled me as well.

"I'm really not trying to be a jerk about this…" I said.

Don't be a condescending ass.

Don't be a condescending ass.

Don't be a condescending ass.

"…but I don't get what the big deal is."

Shit.

"I can't deal with you right now."

Posey pushed herself up from behind her desk. She wasn't showing her pregnancy in the belly yet, but I had noticed she was having a discernible amount of trouble getting in and out of chairs in the last few weeks.

I wanted to say something supportive and also remind her to be safe about the baby and not rush into anything dangerous, but I was running low on spousal respect credits so I told her I loved her and went to visit Parker at the hospital.

• • •

THE HOSPITAL had no record of Parker Farmington as a current patient. They checked again for me, or at least said they did, but still no record. I had a sinking feeling in my gut that all was not well with him and that I wasn't going to be able to stay out of it.

Except that was Dominick Exceptionalism speaking. One thing I'd been trying to focus more on in my writing and my life was not making everything about me. And while this mess swirled all around my periphery, I really had no stake in it. Lindsey and Posey were the characters with agency. Parker and I were scene dressing. The case could be made that I was the designated scribe to relay Lindsey and Posey's adventure to future generations, but I could also make a very good case for just staying the hell out of the way and letting them work through what were obviously complicated issues rather than assuming they needed me to rush in as the hero.

But all that did was leave me more time to go back to a job I hated to support a life I thought was boring and secure but was looking more and more like a façade. So before I went to find Parker, I popped by my boss's office, quit my job, and took my laptop to the campus library to work on my book for the first time in more than three months. I wrote and deleted several chunks trying to move the story forward but eventually realized I had abandoned that book for the same reason I had abandoned helping Posey and Lindsey. I couldn't grasp a family bond strong enough to risk life and career for because I didn't have any strong family bonds myself.

I came from a small, scattered family with no cohesion and a generous helping of Midwestern passive-aggressiveness. I hadn't talked to my parents in more than a year and most days went by without them even passing through my thoughts. And I had no idea how it had gotten that bad and how I had ended up so alone. For the longest time I'd blamed them exclusively and exalted myself as some sort of enlightened survivor for getting out. But with the impending arrival of my first kid to a woman they didn't even know I had married, I realized, finally, how much of the blame I shared and figured it was about time to man up and go see them.

I wanted to jump in the car right then, but before I went to them, I needed to help the closest thing I had to family in Detroit.

Parker Farmington was another person I had misunderstood my connection to and how he had helped me far more than he had hurt me.

It had taken attempted kidnapping and a wild road trip through Canada to knock my head out of my ass and now he was missing and I needed to find him.

Somehow.

Before I could plot my rescue any further, my phone buzzed and I answered. I usually hate talking on the phone and almost always let numbers I don't recognize go to voicemail where their chances of ever being heard again are minimal, but I really had no interest in facing my lack of ability to save Parker, so I answered the phone to distract myself. It was Ellis Meany and he was telling me someone named Jeff Albert had given him my latest manuscript and he wanted to publish it and wondered what else I was working on.

One of the reasons my first novel couldn't be published in the US was because Ellis Meany, a man with too much money, too much bravado, and not enough common sense, bought those rights with a small cash payment and by funding my fellowship with the university. I didn't fully understand all of the paperwork I signed and still had no idea if the way I explained it to people was even true, but I knew Ellis still held out hope to publish a special edition of the book one day that would be printed with ink mixed with blood from myself, Parker, and the serial killer in training we faced off against. With the way things had turned out, I was under the belief the whole thing was brushed aside to eventually be completely forgotten. Apparently I was wrong.

"You remember me, right?" I asked him.

"Bygones, et cetera," Meany said. "No more gimmick publishing for me. Only quality. You've got quality. You and Jeff. I want to do a book with both of you."

My mind was running crazy with the excitement of another potential book deal and freeing up the rights to my first book, so it took a second to realize I had no idea who Jeff Albert was.

"I was with Parker Farmington," I said. "Who is…oh shit. That's where he is."

"Pardon?"

"Yes, I'm very interested in a book deal but I have to go now, I have to save Parker's life."

"Soon, then. We'll talk. We'll sign. I have Japanese whiskey we can drink."

"And yes, I am working on something new. It's more of a caper, a sperm bank robbery."

"That's gross," Meany said.

"I mean it's also about fatherhood and dealing with life after your dreams come true and all of that, but yeah. I think it's going to be driven by a sperm bank robbery."

I hung up and called the hospital to ask if they had a Jeff Albert registered.

• • •

"I THOUGHT they kidnapped you," I told Parker as I handed him a bag of Doritos I bought from the gift shop.

"You need to stop seeing everything in terms of criminal plots."

"The name threw me off," I said.

"It's an awful name."

"And you told me that you changed it after that time at the store but I forgot. I'm an idiot."

"Nobody else knows. Don't feel bad."

Parker and I had crossed paths at an all-night home improvement store last winter and though we'd never admitted it, both of us had been there for suicide supplies. Whether either of us would have ever gone through with it was debatable, but it was enough of a triggering trait to share that we bonded quickly and he'd offered to help me get a writing fellowship in Detroit that matched the one I'd lost in New York City. And he'd shared with me that his real name was Jeff Albert but he changed it to Parker Farmington.

"Ellis Meany knew," I said.

"It's my pen name."

"I'm going to tell my parents about the baby and I'd like you to come with me."

"What about our caper?"

"Lindsey and Posey need to work that out," I said. "We're observers at best, liabilities at worst. I can't help either of them until I understand a family connection deep enough and strong enough to fight over a sperm sample."

"Hmmm."

"You don't have to ride in the trunk this time."

"I've never been to Flint. Could be interesting."

"It's depressing. But they have some good food and you can see the city and the people that made me who I am. That's got to be worth something."

"Unfortunately," he said, waving his hands around the hospital room, "they don't know why I passed out and they want to run more tests."

"You better hope the doctor doesn't refuse to sign off on your final paperwork because he objects to your career path."

Parker smiled, threw the bag of Doritos into the garbage can next to me, and turned the TV on to C-SPAN and waved me off.

• • •

I FELT better driving to Flint knowing that Parker was being taken care of instead of stuck in a kidnapping hole somewhere, but I felt less better about facing my family alone even though it was probably the best way to do it. As I drove I fought consistently to avoid letting a lifetime of slights and parental failures build up in my head and color my conversation. I found a mix of show tunes and sports talk radio was the key to keeping my brain fully occupied. As I came up to the exit to take toward my parents' house in the suburbs, I couldn't bring myself to do it and kept driving.

It had been more than two years since I'd last been home and even then it was just a quick trip directly to my parents' house to say hi to my dad before he went in for heart surgery. The next day I left for a week-long trip to Prague as part of my first attempt at grad school and forgot to call and check on him while he was gone. My foot instinctively pressed down harder on the gas pedal to speed me away from those memories as quickly as possible. When I finally looked down at the speedometer I was going almost 100 miles an hour and realized, once again, I was as much to blame for the interpersonal problems in my life as anyone else even with my family. Especially with my family.

I wasn't interested in thinking anymore about my own fallibility in relationships so I kept driving toward the one place where, for four years at least, I made all the right choices, met all of the right people, and experienced the only bits of success to this point in my life. The Flint campus of the University of Michigan is ugly but charming. The bunker-like design reflected its 1970s construction period, and a lack of imagination in design reflected the lack of faith in the fledgling university's success at the time. But inside, warm tones and a genuinely engaged faculty created an atmosphere of support and joy I had never experienced in my seven other university stops. I worked on the student newspaper, was editor of the student literary magazine, and taught writing to incoming freshmen who needed extra help. I was treated as an equal and as a peer by both my teachers and my fellow students.

Of course, anyone who thinks my talent is overrated would point to this environment as feeding and exacerbating my mediocrity, but all I cared about was the feeling of relief and confidence that overwhelmed me when I walked into the arts and sciences building. I hadn't felt comfortable or confident in a very long time. That feeling didn't last very long. As I stood in the lobby of the building, absorbing all of the emotions, I was ramrodded by a loud group of kids rushing through the door.

"Hey," I yelled toward the center of the group.

Instead of clearing away from me though, the group constricted around me and grew more aggressive in pushing me out of their way. I flopped into one of them, a stocky kid with pasty skin and a T-shirt with an airbrushed eagle riding a bullet. He grunted and pushed me against the brick wall, scraping my arm and drawing blood. I tried to grunt as well but it came out as a scream as I charged him and knocked him to the ground. Immediately I regretted it and expected the group to turn on me, but they bailed on their friend and dispersed quickly, leaving me alone with Mr. Airbrush.

"Sorry, man," I said, holding my hand out to help him up.

He batted it away and stood on his own.

"Watch where you're going next time, old man."

And with eight words that punk in the white trash shirt nailed the biggest problem I had with my life as of late. I was too old for the life I really wanted, and too young and immature for the more mature life options available to me. So I was stuck in the middle biding my time, waiting for a better solution that was becoming increasingly unlikely to show itself. My mood was suddenly sour and I regretted coming to visit. Instead of being excited to go up to the English department floor and brag about my book deal, all I could do was think of ways to be embarrassed by it because it was only digital, it was UK only, it was a crime novel, it was autobiographical, etc. So instead of leaving refreshed and re-energized about my education and my career as I'd hoped, I headed back to my car bitter and resentful, regretting ever signing that deal.

Heading back toward my parents' house, I stopped for Taco Bell as I pulled into town because when I lived there we had to drive almost half an hour away to get Taco Bell. Thinking about that turned out to be a back door for all of the other rotten thoughts to weasel their way in so when I pulled into my parents' apartment complex I had to stop halfway back to their building to throw up my Dorito tacos. This was the first thing my mother commented on.

"You vomit a ridiculous amount," she said. "Even when you were a baby. Throwing up all the time in church. Made me look like I was raising a devil child."

We were sitting on the formal couch in the front room of their apartment. My mom was built, like most of the women in my family, short and wide. She was wearing one of her colorful house dresses and had her good hair in. Along with the boxy frame, my mom and my aunts all had very thin, very blonde hair. While my aunts had gone all-in with the old lady bowl-cut perms, my mom bought extensions from a lady at her church and styled her hair like a televangelist's wife from the '80s. When I was younger her odd look embarrassed me, but as I grew older part of me respected and even envied her individuality.

"Speaking of raising a child," I said, "I have some news."

"Your dad is out getting the groceries. Does he need to hear this? Did you eat?"

"This isn't bad news."

"You never call. This is the first time you've been here since we moved. We could die and I wonder if you'd care."

"Did I ever tell you about Posey? The girl I met from school?"

"You never tell me anything."

"We got married," I said.

Her face lit up in anger and I continued talking before she could build up a full head of hate steam.

"We're having a baby."

"Oh," my mother said. "Sit down. Tell me about her."

"We don't know if it's a girl yet. I don't really have a—"

"Tell me about your wife and why we weren't invited to the wedding."

I wanted to lay it all bare and certainly confess everything I had done wrong but also tear into her about how it was her fault and how she was so judgmental that I didn't even want to bother dealing with excuses. Instead, I said, "I'm sorry. It was kind of a mess and I'm trying to make it better."

She nodded and made some diversionary small talk to see if I would say anything else of import. While we talked, she made me a microwave lasagna and chopped up random vegetables from the fridge that were on the verge of expiration and tossed them into a salad. It didn't matter what she added to the salad because she would top it all off with a thick coating of ranch dressing and it would taste great. When the lasagna was done, my mom screamed for my grandma, who I didn't even know was in the house. My grandma was an older copy of my mother, though neither of them would ever admit it. Her hair was gray and stringy and her house dress was more muted in color. She came hobbling into the kitchen using her trademark sideways shuffle and grabbed a glass from the dishwasher and a TV tray before shuffling out to the family room. I followed her out of the kitchen and watched her put her dentures in the glass on her TV tray and then fiddle around with the remote until Fox News came on. The room was immediately filled with the sound of screaming.

"Hey, Gram," I yelled, trying to be heard over the screeching. "Can you turn that down a second?"

"What?"

"Turn that down. I have something to tell you."

She dug down into the couch to grab the remote again and turned the sound down a few notches. It was still loud, but she was stubborn enough for me to think that was as good as it was going to get. Family trait.

"Why are you here?" she asked.

"I have some news. I just told Mom but—"

"We had a sermon about this the other week at the Salvation Army," she said. "So I'm prepared to love you regardless of your lifestyle."

"My what?"

"Why are you here?"

"I'm having a baby. Well, my wife and I are having a baby."

"Wife?"

I nodded.

"Judy," she yelled to my mother. "Why don't you ever tell me anything?"

My mother didn't answer and my grandma turned the volume back up, indicating the conversation was done. I went back into the kitchen where my mom was pulling a loaf of garlic bread out of the oven. They never used the air conditioning, and between the lasagna and the bread in the oven, it was quickly approaching intolerable levels of heat in the small house.

When my dad came home he immediately dragged me to his office to show me his latest race-walking trophy. He'd been out of racing for a while after coming down with some kind of mysterious illness that plumped him up to almost three hundred pounds but he'd recently regained his fit frame, though the skin around his face hung loose and wobbly. We talked about baseball a bit and what kind of car I was driving. And that was it. There was no breakthrough, no sudden clarity of my place in life. Just one tiny step in a direction I wasn't even sure I wanted to be going in. I hemmed and hawed about any future meetings with Posey or with the baby, but I didn't flat out refuse and I saw that as progress. On the drive home I of course realized the true progress had been facing down the fact I was as much to blame for being estranged from my family as they were. It was an important character moment but when I arrived back home and realized I had been gone almost the entire day, I couldn't really put my finger on how it had helped me move forward in understanding my wife and Lindsey any better.

So I wrote some more. I threw in some magic and monsters to see if that shook anything loose in the plot but ended up deleting it after a few pages. For the time being I was a hero without a story and I didn't like that. I didn't like what it said about my writing that I could only seem to write well when I was facing life-or-death manic adventures, and I didn't like what it said about my personality that I could only be happy in chaos even though I craved stability. It was too late to do much of anything but too early to go to bed, so I changed into some grubby clothes, found a pair of steel-toed boots I'd used a few times when trying to remodel our loft, and I drove out to Titus Wade's old house to see if I could put myself in the pathway of some trouble.

I'd barely made it out of downtown before I was run off the road by the battered old minivan I'd seen in the driveway of the Carter brothers' house.

I should have been more angry about being run off the road but I was pissed that they had lied to me about the van not working and not being able to give me a ride. My displeasure would go unheard, though, because Oranthello pointed a shotgun at me and told me to keep my mouth shut. They zip-cuffed my hands behind my back and I didn't put up a fight.

I was back in the game.

Sure, I was likely the damsel in distress being used as bait for my wife, but I had a defined role and if I was lucky my wits would overcome my stupidity and I'd figure out a way to spin this all into a win. I didn't need to understand family love to succeed, I needed my wife to love me enough to value our future together with our baby over the future of her dead brother. If seeing me kidnapped and distressed was the sort of sappy tear jerking she needed, I was ready and willing. As long as they didn't have plans to torture me.

When we pulled up to Titus's old house, I smiled at the

symmetry of the evening.

"Kind of funny how the night ends, symmetrical like this."

"Why don't you keep your mouth shut," Lemon said, "'fore you piss me off."

"Just making an observation," I said.

"What observation? That we a couple toilet cleaners don't know what a word like symmetrical means?" Lemon asked.

He had an edge in his voice, like he was trying to egg me into a fight.

"You're better than me for cleaning toilets," I said. "Sometimes I think I deserve a job like that more than the cushy jobs I always—"

"Our jobs ain't cushy enough for you now? I'm sick of uppity kids like you mouthing off about—"

"Jesus, man," Oranthello said. "We got more on our plate than a mouthy white boy to worry about."

"Don't like takin' his sass is all."

"Just ignore him."

"I'd rather slap him."

We stayed in the car for what felt like an absurdly long time and that's when my strong resolve started to crack. My imagination took off and unloaded a barrage of painful and deadly scenarios I was certain to be part of. I didn't cry, but I came close. Before I fully cracked, a cell phone rang with a horribly loud ring tone and Lemon grabbed at his crotch and then under his seat before coming up with an honest to god flip phone. He put the phone up to his ear and listened to a voice that was loud enough for me to hear pieces of. When Lemon flipped the phone closed, he whispered something to his brother in hushed but intense tones and Oranthello slammed his hands on the steering wheel before starting the van back up and speeding out of the driveway.

We drove out to their own house and circled the block twice before pulling into the driveway next to the other cars I had been told didn't run. Yes, apparently I was *still* bitter about that. Oranthello opened his door then looked back at me.

"Didn't do your feet 'cause I ain't carrying you," he said.

We walked into the house in silence but their body language was chatty as all hell. Instead of the commanding and domineering personalities they had wielded during our previous meeting, they seemed more desperate and confused. I didn't like that. Desperate men were unpredictable. And the way Lemon was walking mixed with what Oranthello had said over the phone made me think he was hiding some kind of injury that had happened during the theft of the samples from the lab. If he was hiding an injury and he couldn't go to the hospital that made them even more desperate and didn't speak well to my future as a hostage.

"Is this where you're doing the swap with Lindsey?" I asked.

Lemon smacked me again and kicked me in the shins and then punched me in the back.

"Just keep your mouth shut and don't piss him off none," Oranthello said.

"I ain't pissy," Lemon said. "Get your own leg shot up by a lady cop and see who you wanna punch."

"Lindsey shot you?"

"What part of don't piss him off confused you?"

"I knew she was lying to me. She never wanted my help,

she wanted a sucker."

We went inside and Lemon turned on the lights. There was someone sitting on the couch and another figure appeared in the curved doorway leading off to the kitchen. I didn't have a good feeling about these people at all. Once my eyes adjusted to the light and I recognized the men as the prison guards from the hospital I felt even worse.

"I'm going to shoot your brother," the man on the couch said. "I'm going to do it in front of you. And then I'm going to shoot you too."

"The fuck you talking about—"

The man in the doorway pointed a massive revolver at Lemon and shot him twice in the chest. Oranthello screamed and rushed him but the guard on the couch shot him in the leg and the ass, dropping him to the ground where he squirmed and squealed.

"You're going to be the witness," he said to me. "Tell your wife and tell your girlfriend what kind of men we are and why they better not fuck us over."

I nodded and peed my pants.

He stood up and walked to Oranthello.

"I want to believe you were just stupid and didn't know what you were getting into."

"Ffffffffaaahhck. Fuck. Fuck yo—"

The guard shot Oranthello in the head and put his gun away. He waved me over to the couch and motioned for me to sit down.

"You've been following us around," he said.

"I...I don't know—"

"That wasn't a question. You're not very good at what you

do."

"I *don't* do this. That's not me. You've got it all wrong."

"This is not a discussion, goddammit," he yelled. And then he took a few deep breaths and calmed himself down.

"I want to set up a meeting. You'll tell your girlfriend what you saw, explain that if they try anything we will murder all of you."

"She's not my girlfriend," I said. "Lindsey, I mean. We're not even friends but—"

"Just tell them and be very clear about what you saw."

• • •

I WAS terrified, but the guards told me to leave. I'd only ever experienced that level of paralyzing fear in dreams and without being able to wake up to make it stop I had no idea how to function. Standing in the driveway where just a few hours earlier I had roamed freely and arrogantly with a shotgun, I was now soaked in a fog of confusion and panic and depression. I was in mourning for my way of life that had just died and I knew whatever future I was looking on now was a dark one.

I kept walking, no longer afraid of petty vagrants and thieves on the streets. Eventually I made my way to a liquor store where I bought a Snickers bar and a Diet Coke to gin up my energy while I waited for a cab. I tried to call Posey but there was no way to convey what had just happened other than in person.. When I got in the cab the driver stumped me when he asked me where to go. The police station was the obvious destination. I'd been too freaked out to make a proper 911 call but now was the time to bring in the folks who could help, right?

"Let's say I just saw a murder," I said to the driver, a lanky Hispanic guy with patchy hair and a mesh tank top that made him look filthy and trendy all at the same time. "Should I go to the police or—"

"No fucking police or get outta my car. Fucking cops can sit on a fucking chair full of swords, cocksucking asshole motherfuckers."

I had him take me to Posey's office.

Along the way he told me a story about when he was shot during a robbery and it took the police over an hour to show up and when they interviewed him they blamed him for getting shot and took all of his money and put him in jail for weed they found in the backseat. Posey knew the police department and knew her way around the parts that worked properly and protected the city. She'd be the entry point for their involvement. She was also going to be the one who had to lock down Lindsey and keep her from blowing up and getting all of us killed. I was going to be the go-between and hopefully the voice of objectivity and fear-mongering.

Posey was once again gone from the office, which wasn't surprising as a bail officer who sat in the office all day wasn't out making money, so I took the moment to sketch my thoughts out on a steno pad. This was how I'd always worked through complicated issues in my life, even before I officially identified as a writer. In fact, it's likely one of the reasons I became a writer. I was never much of a talker or socializer, I was far too awkward in person for it, but I'd always been able to work out even the most complicated emotional puzzles in scribbles on notepads. Those scribbles eventually became the building blocks of autobiographical poems which grew longer into autobiographical short stories. I was apparently still stuck in the creative trap of only being able to write about my problems, but at that moment, I was happy to have the skill sharp and fresh.

I scribbled and doodled and made lists and did a few lines of stream of conscious thought, looking for a way to unravel the cluster fuck this had become. On paper there was no reason we should even be connected to these correction goons and their mysterious cancer-stricken puppetmaster, but in real life crime tends to operate like a highly contagious disease and folks on the periphery are just as likely to suffer as those in the epicenter. And we were all over the periphery.

If I knew where the money sample really was it would be easy to believe that all we'd have to do was arrange a cordial exchange and everyone would go their own way afterward. And that thinking would end with us lined up next to each other in a weedy lot with a bullet in each of our heads. These guys made their scorched earth no survivor policy quite clear and to survive we were going to need to shut them down, not give them what they wanted. By the time I fell asleep a few hours later I was no closer to a plan than I had been before, but I was a lot closer to believing a plan that would work was possible.

• • •

THE NEXT morning I woke up and sent a text message to Lindsey that I had the real sample they wanted to swap and to meet me at the hospital. I also sent one to Posey that said her doctor called and wanted to see her ASAP. I took the bus over to the hospital and went to see Parker while I waited to hear back from the women in my life. I told him everything that was going on and sketched out a few ideas I had for a way out and he listened silently.

When I was done talking he said, “They’re all pretty stupid ideas, but I don’t think it’s going to be you that gets us all killed.”

“A vote of confidence?”

“Hardly. Least objectionable among bad options, maybe.”

He was watching a History Channel documentary about the building of the Empire State Building and I got sucked in and didn’t realize it was more than an hour before I got a text from Lindsey. I gave her Parker’s room number and told her to meet me. She didn’t want to but I told her it was mandatory. I was hoping to buy enough time to get her and Posey in the same room when I told them what was going on.

“I feel like I’m just moving pieces around on a game board with a toddler,” I told Parker. “It doesn’t matter what I do because it’s all going to end up destroyed on a whim anyway.”

“When I told you it couldn’t end well I wasn’t just talking about myself.”

Lindsey burst into the room before our conversation could get any more fatalistic.

“Let’s get this over with,” she said. “An April baby sounds like a dream.”

She looked at Parker after she said that and they shared an awkward, but not entirely awful, moment and I wondered if there was actually the possibility of them finding a way to work out some kind of weird family arrangement.

“Not just yet,” I said. “We need to talk.”

“Goddammit, what did you do?”

"Just settle down. I'm waiting for Posey to get here. We need to—"

"Oh hell no," she said, spinning away from Parker's bed and rushing me with her finger pointed at my chest.

I put my own hands out to stop her from running over me and barely kept both of us upright while she started swinging at me.

"I knew you were going to mess this up for me. What did you do?"

"Just hold on," I said. "There's more to this tha—"

I expected her to try and hit me again but she let out a high-pitched, primal scream and fell to her knees. It took me a few seconds to realize what she was doing and that it didn't represent any harm to me, but I couldn't stop staring at her. Finally Parker broke my socially awkward trance.

"Is she okay?" he asked.

"Are you okay?" I asked her.

"This is it, what I deserve," she said. "You're what I deserve. *This* is what I deserve."

I held my hand out for her but she slapped it away and struggled back to her feet alone.

"So," I said. "We've kind of got a mess on our hands."

"Whatever," she mumbled. "I've forced it and ridden out fate longer than I should have and it's all just…it's just not meant to be."

"That's all very mature," I said. "But at the moment—"

"Some very bad men want to kill you all," Parker said.

"Come on, man, I wanted to tell them at the same time."

"You're stalling. You have no plan and you're stalling hoping something smart pops into your head before you have to talk. But we all know that's never going to happen. So get everyone on the same page as quickly as possible and..."

His voice dragged off and the beeps on his monitors grew more frantic.

"Parker?"

Lindsey rushed to his bedside and grabbed his face.

"Hey, bucko. Come on back now."

"Ohhhhhhh," he said. "Holy...ughhhhhhh."

"Look what you do to him," she said to me.

I shrugged.

"You said I owe you. I thought I was helping."

A pair of nurses eventually came in to stabilize Parker and bring him back to us while Lindsey and I bickered mindlessly to fill time and keep from focusing too much on the panic setting in. It was more than a half hour later when we realized Posey still hadn't joined us.

"She was smart enough to see through your bullshit," Lindsey said.

"No, something's wrong."

I was sending Posey a barrage of text messages and tried calling her a couple of times. If I thought they would give any sort of helpful information, I'd have called her doctor's office to see if she had checked in with her doctor on her own, but something felt off to me. As high intensity as her career was, she'd worked very hard to keep herself healthy and safe for the baby and had gone to the doctor more since finding out she was pregnant than she had in her entire life before then. Those conversations had gone a long way toward strengthening my feelings for her and for my own conflicted desire for stability and safety in my own life. Even in the midst of some of our worst fights (anyone who thinks having a baby brings couples together needs to talk to more couples) she'd responded quickly to my messages if it had to do with the baby or the doctor. Her silence on this freaked me out.

"Let's get back to bad men wanting to kill us," Lindsey said.

"Shit," I said. "I can't think like this. I can't process this shit."

"You can't process any emotion more complex than potty humor," Parker said. "But I would really love it if you could both maybe take this somewhere else?"

"Shit," I said again. "Right. Sorry. Hey, did they ever figure out what was wrong with you?"

"Go away, please," he said.

Lindsey and I went to the hospital cafeteria and I told her about the guards killing Oranthello and Lemon in front of me and what they told me. She nodded along and ate two giant bowls of the most disgusting oatmeal I'd ever seen in my life. I ate two plain donuts and a package of cartoon-shaped fruit snacks. We shared a large Diet Coke because they were running low on cups and neither of us cared for diet soda out of plastic bottles.

"And we don't know where the sample they want is?"

I shook my head.

"It could still be in the lab for all we know, which is why those two couldn't find it when they were there and took ours instead. I think they lied about there being trouble in the lab and just took Titus's sample and hoped to squeeze us for the same amount."

"The whole thing stinks to me and I think there's more to it than what they told you."

"So what do we do?"

She finished the last of her oatmeal and sucked down the rest of the soda, swishing it around in her mouth before answering.

"Find the guards and blow their fucking fingers off until they tell us what we need to know."

I nodded, looked to see if there was a restroom nearby, and then threw up on the floor.

I followed behind Lindsey as we headed toward where she parked her car, trying to explain to her why hunting these prison guards down was an incredibly bad idea. She was blinded by…I don't even know…it seemed to range from disgust to fear to love and not open to anything approaching rational discussion. But I also knew she was right, that our options were limited, and if I was going to be hunted down by deadly killers I was likely better off with her than on my own. I just hoped my eventual death would be fast and sudden and I wouldn't have to face any kind of torture.

"I want to find Posey first," I said. "This isn't like her to disappear and we need her. *You* need her."

"Absolutely not."

"You didn't see these guys. They were ruthless."

"They didn't kill you."

"I was the messenger."

Lindsey stopped walking but didn't turn around. I ran into

her and bounced backward and almost fell on my butt.

"What the—"

"The best thing you can do for your pregnant wife," Lindsey said, still facing away from me, "is help me find these guys and take them out before they can cause any more trouble."

"I don't have any special skills or special knowledge," I said. "So why do you even want me around?"

This time she did turn around. The conversation to that point had hints of menace, but the next five words out of her mouth absolutely dripped contempt and cruelty.

"I need you for bait."

I had to give her points for honesty at least. And even knowing that, part of me still thought staying with Lindsey was the better option because even as bait I was likely safer with her than I was on my own. But I couldn't get Posey out of my head. I've never been masculine in the traditional sense, but I was driven by a need to protect my wife and my potential child in a way I'd never been driven by anything else in my life. I'd been trying to play both sides of the loyalty fence but it was time to make a choice. And I was team Posey.

"If I'm going to be bait for anyone," I said, "it's going to be for my wife."

She didn't try to change my mind. I felt bad for her, not because she was losing a partner or losing her bait, but because she was lonely enough and desperate enough to see someone as useless as myself as her only ally. When she was gone, I looked around at where I was and wished I'd caught a ride with Lindsey to someplace more convenient before I abandoned her. But the hospital held its own advantages so there were certainly worse places I could have been left. I'd quit my job, but I knew enough about the slow processing time for paperwork in the hospital to suspect my login credentials were still valid. My office was off limits, certainly, but I knew the medical library they had just remodeled had plenty of computer terminals as well as enough privacy to function as a satellite base for my rescue operation.

Despite Parker's and Lindsey's hints that Posey's silence was proof of her abandonment and betrayal of me, I wasn't convinced. We had a volatile relationship and there were certainly secrets and a bit of mistrust between us, but that was mostly due to our divergent career paths rather than any sort of marital rift. Our marriage was solid and bonded by genuine love, no matter how odd and corny it looked to outsiders.

Unfortunately, trust and love wasn't going to help me find my wife. I needed to go all in on the distrust and suspicious part of our relationship. All of the tracking options she had for me worked in reverse, though I'd never had need to use them. I tried her phone first, hoping to get lucky, but I knew every time she got a new iPhone, the first thing she did was turn off the GPS and the Find My Phone feature. So while I could get a general sense of where she was, I couldn't get the street-level specifics that were available with the GPS on.

I was happy to see that sensors did indicate she was still in the metro Detroit area and she hadn't skipped town or anything, but to get what I needed I had to crack into the GPS unit in her truck. She had the same tracking sensors in her vehicles that I had disabled in my own car, but I didn't bother trying hers. She'd be smart enough to turn it off or remove it completely if she went off the grid and I had a better option anyway.

The GPS unit she had was a detachable one that could move

between vehicles. I'd taken it once on a road trip and had trouble with it and needed to contact the manufacturer with the serial number. I still had that number in a note on my phone in case I ever needed it so I typed it in on the manufacturer's website and after a few tries for Posey's password, I was able to log into the back end of the unit where I could not only see in real time where the unit was, I could also access the search history and see what addresses she'd typed in previously to build a profile of what she was up to. The first thing I checked was the unit's location and noted the cross streets. I was disappointed that I didn't recognize the area and didn't see anything in the search history that jumped out at me. The optimist in me had been hoping for something obvious and easy but the realist in me was having fun pointing out how stupid that had been.

The realist was also pointing out that no matter how useful any information was I could retrieve, the lack of car nearby was going to be a pretty big pain in my ass. I was running possible options through my head from laziest to most depressing when I remembered an offer from Zipcar I'd seen in my student email recently. I clicked the logo that let me download the app to my phone so I could check in on it from the road then logged back into my email, signed up for the free Zipcar trial, and found out there was a car within a block of where I was. I was pleased to see the linked page automatically filled with all of my campus contact information, including the PO # attached to my fellowship. That would make it harder for anyone to track me through credit or debit card usage and would also alleviate the issue of me needing to check any card I put in to make sure it had enough available to cover my expenses. Of course I didn't breathe until I clicked submit and the transaction was complete.

Thus is the life of the modern creative class.

Fifteen minutes later I wandered out into the blocks surrounding the hospital that I'd never been into on foot in search of a shiny new car that would inevitably stick out among the rusted beaters and student specials that populated the area. I found it quickly in a red, white, and blue Mini Cooper. Not just too new and shiny for the area, but too foreign. It embarrassed me after the fact, but I couldn't help but wonder how many cars the company lost to theft and carjackings in a given month. Because of this thought, I found myself hyperaware of my surroundings, which is why I noticed the Department of Corrections van coming my way with enough time to duck off behind a building to watch it pass by.

The path the van was traveling was common enough for all of the corrections vehicles so there was no reason to assume it was the murderous guards coming to look for me but I was in no mood to risk it. I hated being in a defensive position with these guys, always looking behind me or in front of me, always being afraid. I thought to myself how much easier it would be if I knew their boss's schedule so I'd know when they were all going to be at the hospital together and, more importantly, occupied with tasks other than murdering me and my friends. And then I realized that even more important than my hospital Internet access was my access to the cancer center scheduling system. Accessing it for this purpose was against any number of health system and departmental guidelines as well as violating federal HIPAA laws, but my survival at the moment trumped all of that and it would be a whole lot easier to fight criminal charges when this was over than it would be to fight death if these assholes murdered me.

Getting back into the hospital was harder this time because I had to find a machine that was connected to the health system's secure network because that was the only way to access the scheduling system. The best computer would have been at my desk in the sperm lab or one of the other desks in my old office, but after telling off my boss and my coworkers, that was less of an option. I wandered the hallways waiting for inspiration to strike while also looking out for murderous prison guards. It wasn't the best environment for success, but it distracted me enough that I missed the bright yellow cones marking off where the cleaning crew had just mopped the floor.

My right foot hit the wet floor first and slipped out from underneath me. To try and balance myself, I dug my left foot into the floor and that's when I felt my knee pop. Luckily it wasn't anything major and I was able to shake it off and keep walking. Even better, it gave me an idea. My lack of coordination was legendary in my department and twice during the previous winter I'd ended up in the employee health clinic after wiping out on wet floors. My experiences gave me two great pieces of intel: 1) each of the clinic rooms had kiosk machines that were connected to the secure system and 2) they were pretty free with who they let access those kiosks because they knew employees needed to have access to email to keep up on work during the interminable wait to see a doctor.

I had a moment of panic when the clerk told me she couldn't find me in the system.

"I always have this problem," I said.

She glared at me with eyes that were intensified by thick glasses and thick, black eyeliner. The only bit of color on her was a small rainbow pin with the word ALLY written above in golden script.

"You have a chronic issue?"

"Chronic clumsiness," I said.

She rolled her eyes this time and clicked and clacked around her system a bit longer until she found information satisfactory enough to let me in.

"We're not really set up for chronic conditions," she said.

"The ER freaks me out," I said. "Over here is more relaxing. Less...hospital if you will."

She waved me over to the waiting room without making eye contact this time.

"Psych ward might be more your fit next time," she mumbled under her breath as I walked away.

And I couldn't let it go.

I was almost in. Great idea executed with precision.

"Excuse me?" I said.

"Someone will be with you soon."

"You think I like this shit?"

"We don't tolerate language like that in this clinic."

Deep breath. Don't blow this, dumbass.

"But they'll tolerate..."

Happy place. Almost there.

"...I'm sorry," I said. "It's just this pain in my leg is killing me and I'm trying to wrap up this big project for my department's Pride Week celebration and I'm waiting on this important email from a vendor and I can't check my email because I refuse to download the new software to my phone that's nothing but a privacy grab and—"

"Isn't that the worst?" she asked.

Wait. What? This is good.

"Like checking my work email on my phone isn't demoralizing enough, we have to sign over any shred of privacy we might have retained."

"A friend of mine heard from someone whose work did this and she typed the wrong password into her phone and it erased everything."

"I just wish there was a way to check my email over here so I could relax and know this thing has been taken care of."

This time we locked eyes and she didn't look away or roll her eyes. After a long pause, she looked back down at her keyboard.

"I've got to go make some copies," she finally said. "Why don't you check your mail here while I'm gone."

I thanked her with something approaching genuine appreciation and settled in to find what I was looking for. But I wasn't able to catch a break. Even though I was still able to log into the network and access the web and my email, my access to the patient records system, of which the scheduling program was a key part, had been terminated. I'd made it this far and was in no mood to give up, so I pushed the bounds of ethical justification a bit further and logged in with my manager's credentials.

Once in, it didn't take me long to get into the system and, even though I didn't know the name of the patient I was looking for, I knew the code language the schedulers used to indicate to all involved with the appointment that it was a prisoner and special preparation would be needed. There was only one patient in the system with those comments, which made my job easier. I printed off a copy of his schedule for the next week and as I was cramming it into my pocket I looked at the patient's name again. Morton Taylor. It rang a bell but I couldn't place it right away. When I eventually did place it, my stomach dropped and my asshole clenched. It was even worse than I could have imagined.

I logged off and was out of the employee health clinic before the clerk returned. The schedule I needed was in my pocket but I didn't feel as triumphant as I had hoped. In addition to the treatment schedule for the gangster patient trying to kill me, I had his name: Morton Taylor. I assumed it was senior because I had once known Morton Taylor, Junior. I was next to him on a street in Toledo, Ohio, when my wife shot him to death.

Posey hadn't been my wife at the time and I only knew him as a nut job named Rickard who saw me as some kind of creative muse for his budding career as a serial killer. He killed her brother and she stabbed a syringe in his throat before shooting him in the head. It was a visual that haunted me in my sleep and unfortunately even in the bedroom with Posey. The sound of the syringe going into his neck and the blast of gunshot were an echo I couldn't escape and was the real reason I didn't have any interest in pursuing my wife's career. And now it was haunting me in real life too.

Walking back to my Zipcar, I screamed as loudly as I could into the sky and shook the scheduling printout. I hated to admit that the clerk's comment about me needing to go to the psych ward was probably on target. But first I had to save my wife. Or attempt to save my wife. Or at least find her and be close enough to her when the shit rained down that I could catch a lucky break and survive. Or I could call Lindsey with the information I had and hope to god siding with her didn't come back and bite me. I stared at my phone in my hand for a long time trying to figure out what to do next.

"I know where the guards are going to be tomorrow," I told Lindsey when she answered her phone.

"Goddammit, you son of a…I don't even know how to take that. I'm out here at the brothers' house and it's like they were never here. So I'm just wondering what my next step should be when—"

"I've got a car," I said. "A Zipcar, through the school, I'm coming out to you."

"I don't like the sound of that at all."

"Me either," I said. "See you in a few."

A few turned out to be thirty minutes because I got lost. Again. But she was still there, her cruiser parked in the driveway and her on the porch swatting at mosquitoes.

"This is the fucking city," she said when I laughed at her. "You shouldn't have to deal with this shit in the city."

I pointed to the swampy pond down the road from the house where the scattered remains of three burned out houses remained.

"This isn't your average city."

She waved me inside and to the couch while she leaned

against the doorway between the living room and the kitchen stretching her arms.

"I've got this cramp that just—"

"I gotta get out of here," I said.

I went back out to the porch where fending off mosquitoes was better than fending off the look of confused horror on Oranthello's face right before his head exploded. Swatting away that thought brought another to mind. I knew who the patient was, but I had no idea who the guards were. I wondered if that made any kind of difference.

"What the hell was that?" Lindsey asked from behind the screen door.

"Isn't it dangerous to have your cruiser out where everyone can see it?"

"This is my job," she said. "I'm running down leads for the investigation into a campus larceny."

"Huh," I said. "Do you know who the guards are who are trying to kill us?"

"Where does that come from? Why are you asking about my cruiser and who I know?"

I tried to maintain eye contact with her while I pondered her skittish paranoia. Our interactions together, though intense and life-altering, didn't really add up to much time-wise. But in the small sample size, I'd seen her exhibit a strong degree of genuine fear that everyone was out to get her and that her entire life was always just a moment away from being snatched away from her. I'm sure there was a great character study in there somewhere about her and that as a writer I could build a wonderful, complex, and flawed heroine, but right then, I couldn't tell if she was being her normal level of paranoid or if she was using it as a distraction or cover to hide something from me.

"I'm just working this stuff out in my head," I said. "I just wondered…I mean don't these corrections guys have to coordinate with the campus or hospital police or something?"

"Does it matter what their names are? Do you want to send them gifts? Engraved invitations?"

"I do know one name," I said, somehow eager now to please her and justify my line of questioning. "Morton Taylor."

"Jesus Christ," she sighed. "Let's not bring up that loon again."

"Senior," I said, letting the word hang in the air until she caught on.

"Oh shit."

"I know, right?"

She flung open the screen door and grabbed the scheduling printout from me.

"Shit," she said. "Shit shit shit."

"You're not one for verbal variety, are you?"

She punched me in the head with the paper and then stuck it under my eyes.

"Does your wife know about this?"

"I don't know. *I* just found out."

"But she's smarter than you."

"So are you," I said. "And you didn't know."

"How far back does this go, do you think? Was it ever about his swimmers or is this some kind of cocked up revenge scheme?"

I shrugged.

"You think the Carter brothers were in on it?"

She was looking down at the paper now, I assumed trying to divine more information from it than was printed.

"Would make sense why they killed them. Loose ends and all," she said.

"There's no way out of this. They're going to kill us all."

And as I said it, I was shocked to find a sense of relief wash over me. I wouldn't have to find a way to solve the problem. I wouldn't have to play hero. I wouldn't have to face the consequences of poor life choices or face the complex decisions ahead of me. I'd wasted the chances I'd been given and there was nothing in my personality or life history to indicate I'd do any better with a second or third chance, so it only seemed fair.

"Don't say that. Don't spin that fatalistic bullshit that Parker likes so much. We can do this. We will survive and we *will* succeed."

"We need to get Posey. We need to do this together for any chance at pulling it off. This split up Scooby-Doo crap is going to get us all killed."

Lindsey grabbed my face and I honestly thought she was going to bite me, but instead she smiled. And then she laughed a deep belly laugh and squeezed my cheeks.

"I may turn you into a baller yet."

"The schedule has Taylor and the guards at the hospital tomorrow at nine a.m. He'll be on the table for about thirty minutes and then they'll be back on the road. Guards can't be in or around the treatment or waiting rooms during treatment so they usually go upstairs to the cafeteria."

She looked down at her watch then said, "It's almost three p.m., that gives us about eighteen hours to find your wife before we have to be at the hospital. Where do we start?"

I held up my phone.

"I can track the GPS box she's using in her car."

"You seem stupid enough to get caught like that, she seems smarter."

"She has to have it on because it's the only way she knows how to get around the city. There's a back way into it that she doesn't know I know about."

I opened the app on my phone; the serial number for Posey's device was already saved so it opened right up to the map and the dot where she was. Lindsey recognized the area and ran to her car.

"No," I said. "We take mine. You're not a cop anymore on this."

"Bullshit I'm not. It's the only advantage I have. If you don't want to ride with me you can follow me."

I looked at the car I had already paid a deposit for and wasn't keen on leaving it where it was. The Zipcar contract included insurance, but I didn't want to deal with the hassle if it was damaged or stolen. I'd also been burned too many times by not having a car around when I eventually pissed off whoever was driving me, so I told her I'd drive myself.

Since I had the GPS tracker, it was easier for me to know exactly where we were going and I arrived first. It was a really rough neighborhood out on the Dearborn border and I saw Posey's car in the middle of the street when I turned the corner. My brain was processing that weird visual as Lindsey pulled up behind me and honked her horn. A split second later Posey's car exploded.

I didn't have even a second to process the explosion when two men with machine guns and two with handguns appeared in my periphery and began firing at Posey's car. Lindsey was out of her car and firing at the group before I had even put my car in park. The wave of gunfire swung away from Posey's car toward my car and Lindsey's. I didn't have a gun and even if I did, I'd be cut down by gunfire before I could get a shot off. Then, for a brief second, real life gave me a leg up over fiction. In movies, machine guns fire endlessly but in real life, a gun on full automatic goes through a clip very quickly. When they stopped to reload at the same time I drove my car at them. Turns out I had a bit of a protective instinct in me after all.

The gunmen turned to look at me, though I can't imagine they were all that threatened by an approaching Mini, no matter how fast I was going, but I tried to compensate for the size of the car by swerving it back and forth, hoping to knock them over like armed bowling pins. I was able to knock one of them down before he could reload and Lindsey used the distraction to approach and take out another one with her shotgun. I kept driving then slammed on the brakes and threw it into reverse. Actually, it was less dramatic than that as this model had a push button transmission, but going backward I was able to take out the remaining gunman.

These guys didn't seem very good at what they did, but even piss-poor shots were bound to get lucky eventually with that kind of firepower. Lindsey caught three rounds in the chest that blew her backward onto the ground. That seemed to be what they wanted because the remaining two gunmen scattered to a waiting car and sped away. I tried to get a look at the license plate, but couldn't focus and was more concerned with checking on Lindsey. The shots hit her in her body armor, but I knew that was still a pretty rough blow to take. She was conscious and breathing when I got to her. I helped her get her vest off and checked to make sure none of the rounds had nicked her under the arm or any other vital place. Everything looked good so I reached out my hand to help her stand up but she waved me off with a groan.

"Check her car," she moaned.

I looked around to see if any of the gunmen had returned, but the street was clear so I checked in the driver's seat hoping not to see Posey's body but expecting the worst. But there was nobody in the car. That didn't make any sense. And then it did make sense and I freaked out. What if it was nothing more than some bored hoodlums destroying a car for fun? Then Lindsey and I just took out a bunch of innocent people.

Shit shit shit.

If they were just fooling around though, why did they have

Posey's car? Had she been carjacked? I tried not to think about carjackings so much, but the news had me convinced it was a danger every time I drove in the city. My socially improper thoughts were interrupted by a muffled banging coming from the trunk.

No.

The car wasn't burned as badly as I thought with the explosion concentrated mostly at the front of the car, but the passenger area was still burning, making it impossible to get at the keys in the ignition so I didn't have any way to get the trunk open. The fire was quickly moving toward the back of the car and I didn't expect to have much time to evaluate my options before the flames hit the gas tank. Lindsey's police cruiser would have help for both problems.

I popped open the cruiser's trunk and quickly found a fire extinguisher in a holster off to the right side, but I had more trouble finding something to pry open Posey's trunk with. A crowbar would have been the best thing to find, but I would have settled for even one of those blackjacks they use to unlock doors for stupid people like me who lock their keys in the car all the time. My luck turned when I pulled the spare tire out of the top shelf of the trunk organizer and found a bar with a lug wrench at one end and a flat blade at the other. It was as close to a crowbar as I was going to get.

Back at Posey's car I sprayed the fire down with the extinguisher and with that danger dissipated I went to work on the trunk with the pry bar. It took me longer than I expected and instead of the lock popping I think I ended up just smashing it loose. Posey was tied up in the back with a rag duct taped into her mouth. I mustered every bit of adrenaline in my body to get her out of the trunk and flopped her down onto the street next to Lindsey.

"Can you get up?" I asked Lindsey.

She wiggled around and tried to get up on her own while I untied Posey and tried to get the gag out of her mouth without ripping the tape off. No luck on either front. The tape was wrapped all the way around her head and I had to rip at her hair to get it loose. When she was finally free I helped Lindsey stand up and then supported her while she regained her normal breathing. Posey was able to stand on her own as well.

"Hospital then?" I asked.

They both shook their heads no. I needed them both at full strength, though, and didn't think waiting for them to heal up under the protective eye of the hospital where we needed to be in the morning anyway was such a bad idea. I briefly considered calling 911 and having an ambulance take us all, but I didn't want to deal with police questions and I was pretty sure they both felt that way as well. Pulling up to the ER entrance in my car with a banged up front and back end gave us good cover for a story about being hit by a driver who sped away and left us injured and disoriented.

Posey and Lindsey were whisked away and I was left with my thoughts and my indestructible Y chromosome in the waiting room. Later in the afternoon like this, the waiting room was empty and the TV was tuned to *Judge Judy*. Posey liked to watch shows like *Judge Judy* and those horrible paternity test talk shows because she said they made her feel better about her life no matter how screwed up it got. I watched a mother suing her daughter over a car loan and wondered how things had spun so wildly out of control with my marriage. I wanted to put a stop to it and go find a cop and tell him everything and bring the full weight of the law down on these goons who were screwing with my life. But I'd seen too many good people with bad luck or okay people with good intentions and poor judgment end up sacrificed to the gods of justice to trust anyone in a uniform other than Lindsey. So I watched TV, kept my mouth shut, and waited to hear from a doctor about when we could all leave.

• • •

WE CHECKED out of the hospital the next morning at six a.m. with a healthy report on the baby for Posey, a handful of prescriptions for Lindsey, a suspicious look from the nurse for all of us, and absolutely no idea of what to do next. Posey was frustratingly silent about what she'd been up to on the side and Lindsey was high on violent fantasies and revenge schemes. Rational thought was hard to come by and I was certainly no source for it. So we talked it out over hospital bagels and more flat diet soda from the cafeteria.

"We can't just go in there and shoot them, right?" I asked.

"They blew away two guys right in front of you. Maybe we just turn them in and let the law take care of them," Lindsey said.

Posey grunted. It was the most communication we'd gotten from her since arriving at the hospital. I tried not to let my mind wander to the worst thoughts of what could have happened to her (and selfishly what that would mean for me) but it wasn't working. I needed something to occupy me and consume me.

"We go to the head," I said, "not the arms."

"Taylor?"

Posey's face twitched when Lindsey said the name.

"You know, don't you?" I asked.

Posey nodded.

I put my hand on her leg and squeezed and was happy when she didn't push it away. The only thing that would have made it better was a monologue from her about what she'd been up to when she wasn't with me, but I knew her well enough to know that wasn't forthcoming. It wasn't a lack of respect or a lack of trust, it was a long-held family trait of stubborn silence and the desire to fix problems solo. It had rarely been a problem in our daily married life—she sought out my input and gave me a running commentary on many things—but it was going to be a big problem as we tried to get out of the current mess. I was also slightly jealous of anyone with the control to stay quiet longer than ten seconds and not talk everything out.

"So we go talk to him then?" Lindsey asked.

Posey shook her head, more face twitching, and then I saw something I thought I would never see: Lindsey soften up to Posey.

"What happened out there?" she asked. "You know my story, right?"

She nodded.

"Can't let that shit bubble underneath, gotta let it out or it'll turn you into a bitter old bat like me."

I looked back at Posey for another acknowledging facial expression or grunt, but nothing. I waited for Lindsey to say something else, but again, nothing. I sat there in awkward discomfort for ages before Posey finally spoke.

"I told him," she said, pointing at me, "and I'll tell you the same thing. It. Isn't. Always. About. You."

Lindsey smirked and rolled her shoulders. I waited for more information but Lindsey and Posey stood up, ready to leave.

"Wait, no," I said. "What in the hell is that supposed to mean? You didn't answer my calls or my texts, I find you bound and gagged in the trunk or your burning car, and all I get is, it's not about me?"

"I ordered a bigger coffee than I normally do. I also had a smaller bag because I expected to be running around in the street a lot today."

WTF?

Lindsey didn't seem to be as confused and appalled by this weird misdirection as I was and that made me even more angry.

"I don't even…what does that have to do with—"

Posey put her right hand over my mouth and reached into her purse with the other and pulled a sticky iPhone out.

"I spilled coffee on my phone. It stopped working. I got in over my head at work, maybe pushed too far on something and…well, thank you for helping me. That's it."

Lindsey held up her arm and pointed at her watch.

"Fifteen minutes. Are we going to see Taylor or not?"

"It can't hurt to talk to him," I said. "And that's the only chance we'll have to talk to him. We talk to him and then we know where we stand."

We both looked at Posey for her response.

"This is not about him," she said.

"Right now it's about these guards," I said. "Maybe we talk to them. Maybe we get them to admit what they did on record and turn that over to the cops and then we're done."

"Just shove a microphone in front of their face and say 'hey, would you mind confessing to multiple premeditated murders right here and now?'"

"I don't know. No. That's stupid. But we've spent so much time wandering around looking over our shoulders and chasing other people, this is our chance to go on the offensive for once."

"Look at you, Mr. Alpha Male," Posey said, smiling. "But I can't look at him. I just...go without me."

"I'll stay with her," Lindsey said. "You go in and get what you can out of him."

This new sensitive and trusting Lindsey was freaking me the hell out, but I knew I had a small window of opportunity here and wasn't going to argue even if I suspected it would come back and smack me in the long run.

My manager was rarely ever in the clinic—she had the same squicky feelings about being around patients as I did—so I wasn't really afraid of a confrontation with her when I went down to find Taylor. I was concerned that with the rotating shifts of the radiation therapists, no one who owed me a favor would be working Taylor's treatment. I got down to the basement where all of the radiation treatment rooms were located just in time to see Taylor being wheeled from the waiting room into the treatment vault. Two guards were with him as dictated by protocol, but they weren't the two guards who had threatened me.

When Taylor was safely inside the vault, I ducked into the control room that I was pleasantly surprised to see was stocked with therapists who liked me. I gave them a brief and innocent rundown of what I was looking for and asked about the guards. They were busy with their prep, so I didn't get much out of them except to find out the two guards with him now were the guards who had been with him since the beginning of his treatment, and the two guys I described sounded a lot like Taylor's two older sons who had a habit of causing disturbances when they were around and had been banned from the department.

I thanked them, offered them lunch sometime, and went to find Posey and Lindsey to share my news. On the way to the cafeteria, I saw the two, dressed in the corrections department uniforms as always, getting out of the elevator opposite me. My first instinct was to confront them with what I had just learned and see how the situation played out. I'd read enough detective novels to know a standard trick of the PI was to egg the bad guys into a confrontation in a public place and get them so worked up they did something stupid that would get them arrested. But I was no detective hero, so I found the nearest hospital police officer and pointed to the pair.

"Those guys are murderers and they're impersonating corrections officers," I told him.

He looked across the hall at them and then at me with a look of bored contempt.

"Very funny. Please move along."

"I work here. I used to work here. My name is Dominick Prince and those guys are—"

"You need to come with me," the officer said, grabbing my wrist.

"No, I'm serious, they're relatives of a cancer patient and—"

"Be quiet and come with me or I'll have to—"

"Hey, assholes," I screamed loudly toward them. "I know you're not really corrections officers."

They might have been ruthless. They might have been tough. But they were not smart. Because they turned around to look at me.

"See," I said to the hospital officer. "Why would they turn around if—"

"You broke into our patient information system and accessed private data against federal guidelines."

"I what?"

Had the clerk from the clinic turned me in or was someone tracking my access? Or was Taylor's record under surveillance? I didn't like that thought at all.

"So many lies you can't keep it all straight," he said. "I see one of your kind every month around here. Trying to make an extra buck by selling—"

"Wait. No. I wasn't trying to do anything wrong. This is a big misunderstanding."

"That you can explain to the detectives."

I wanted to say more and protest my case, but it wasn't going to do me any good. It was time to exercise my right, if not my ability, to remain silent until I came across someone who understood what was happening and could help me. But as I saw the two fake guards walking away, I was overcome instead by the same instinct that made me drive into a crowd of armed goons with my rental car: I ran. I wanted to run after the guards, but I knew that would only make things worse. I needed to get out of the hospital and regroup with Posey and Lindsey to discuss the new information about our friend Morton Taylor so I ran away from the guards, toward the back half of the hospital where the cancer center was and where I would have a territorial advantage over the cop who would likely only be familiar with the main artery floors of the hospital. A year of slacking off from work and spending hours wandering through the hidden halls of the hospital made it almost ridiculously easy to lose the cop on my tail after just a few minutes. It wouldn't take him long to rally other officers to seal off the exits so I needed to work quickly. Getting out to the ER exit where my car was parked seemed like a no-go. What I really needed was a vehicle they wouldn't be looking for me in. And that's when I thought of Ethan Hall and his endless requests to take me on a helicopter ride.

"How about that chopper ride?" I asked without preface.

He didn't hesitate, didn't ask any questions, just grabbed his jacket, smacked me on the back, and led me out to the helipad.

"We were just about to take it out for a test ride," he yelled at me over the already deafening sound of the blades warming up. "Nice timing."

I nodded and gave him a thumbs-up for no particular reason. There was another guy already behind the controls, which made me happy because Ethan never seemed like the pilot sort to me.

"It's okay if I come with?"

Ethan nodded and smacked the pilot on the back.

"Jasper here owes me a pile of favors. He's good for this. Don't worry."

Nobody asked why I was suddenly interested in a helicopter ride and I didn't volunteer any information toward that end. I just enjoyed the ride and let my brain wander and my subconscious do some of the heavy lifting for a bit. Things were going great and I was feeling a sense of organized calm overcome me before it all went to hell over a cemetery along Woodward Avenue.

The helicopter lurched to the right, the pilot cursed, and we wobbled a bit before the helicopter lurched backward.

"What the hell was that?" I asked.

"What the hell was that?" Ethan asked the pilot.

The pilot ignored us both as he was occupied with keeping the helicopter in the sky. He failed and after spinning completely around more than once, the chopper dropped and my seat belt dug into my lap while my back snapped into a twisted arch and my head whipped backward. The chopper banked to the right and my whole body went with it, sending me crashing into an instrument drawer, spraying scalpels and needles through the cabin. There was one more drop that pushed me back into place, bruised and disoriented, then we went down in the cemetery.

It was over quickly and at first I was surprised how much fun it turned out to be once I realized I wasn't dead. But when the ringing in my ears wouldn't stop and when my knees buckled every time I tried to stand, I realized I was in pretty bad shape. I hadn't thrown up, which, frankly, concerned me more than anything. The only good thing I could cling to about the ordeal so far was that I was far away from the hospital and its nosy police officer.

"So, man, uh, this is hard to bring up now and all that," Ethan stuttered. "But we gotta call a response crew out here for this and it would be cool if maybe...you know—"

"I don't want to be here when they show up," I said. "Don't worry about it."

Ethan smiled wide and bobbed his head.

Cool, man. Thanks. We'll have to get up again when maybe it doesn't shit out on us."

I told him sure and though I was aching and my vision was blurry and I probably had internal injuries I wouldn't find out about for weeks, I walked away from a helicopter crash, which is something I truly never thought would factor into my life. And once again, despite renting a car this time, I was left on the edge of the city, stranded.

I didn't remember Posey's phone wasn't working until I tried calling it three different times. Lindsey answered on the first ring and didn't seem at all interested in what I had learned or how I had ended up miles away in a cemetery.

"Why are the cops here looking for you?" she asked.

"Come and get me and we can go over all of this. I found out some—"

"This isn't so easy now. You jacked it up five ways to Sunday with whatever you did on the computers."

"You knew I got the schedule," I said.

"I didn't know you did it illegally."

"Because you're suddenly the moral center of this adventure?"

"I don't care about your morals, jackass, I care about you making it harder for me to do my job and still keep up with this other stuff."

"Just come and get me," I said. "Is Posey still with you?"

Pause.

"Posey said no."

I slammed the phone down and hoped she was joking and would come and pick me up. The seriously tall Arabic man behind the front desk in the cemetery's office scolded me for damaging the phone and asked me for a hundred bucks to cover purchasing a new handset.

"No cash," I said. "Wife doesn't trust me."

He didn't find that humorous. I tried to leave and go wait out front for Lindsey to come and pick me up but the man wouldn't budge. He pointed to the phone and demanded money in a very thick Middle Eastern accent.

I held my hands up in the universal sign for being broke and he reached under the counter and pulled out a handgun: the universal sign for overreacting.

"Five dollars."

"I'm going for my wallet," I said. "Okay?"

He nodded but kept the gun pointed at my center of mass while I slowly reached around and pulled my black wallet with the glow-in-the-dark Batman logo out of my pocket and tossed it onto the counter in front of him. He took the wallet and thumbed through it, finding the cash Posey had given me earlier that I had forgotten about until just then. I expected him to let me go after that but he put the wallet down and kept the gun pointed at me.

"You lied to me."

"I forgot about that. It's a weird—"

"Follow me."

I grabbed my wallet and cash from the counter and followed him. My first instinct was to run, but I wasn't sure how accurate he was with the gun and had no interest in finding out the hard way. So I followed him out through the back door of the small office to the parking lot where a group of men were gathered around a tractor loading supplies into a small trailer.

"Few diggers today," the man said. "You dig with them. One hour, one hundred dollars."

"Wow, really?"

That would be the most money I'd ever made at a job and it was kind of a sobering realization. I really wanted to be out front waiting for Posey or Lindsey, but I also was in no mood to continue arguing with this man and I was intrigued by the opportunity to focus on a hard and manual task for a while rather than worrying about my impending death at the hands of Morton Taylor. The man from the office waved over one of the men, a stocky fellow with a shaved head and a thick beard, and spoke to him in a rapid Middle Eastern language I didn't recognize while pointing at me every few words. When he was done talking, I was led by my new bearded friend over to the tractor where he introduced me to everyone as Joe.

"Dominick," I said. "Not Joe. My name isn't Joe."

My bearded friend shrugged.

"I'm Saul, you'll be digging with me. Doesn't really matter what the rest of them think your name is, does it?"

"No, I guess not."

We ended up at the back of the cemetery where a green tent was set up over a plot of dirt. I assumed this was where our hole was going to go. In retrospect I realize I missed a great opportunity to quiz this man about his job and pick up interesting insights I could use in future writing work, but at the time I was eager to get a shovel and dig until my brain was clear. It was one more reminder that I didn't have the drive needed for writing, or the focus to take advantage of the opportunities afforded to me, and I was far too flaky and precious to make any sort of inroads in the traditional job world. That, more than anything else, was why I was not writing in New York City as had long been my dream and why I kept finding myself torn between the dying sparks of my romanticized idea of the writing life and my romanticized view of a workaday blue collar life.

So I dug a hole. I wasn't very good at it and my poor technique aggravated the pain in my back and legs from the crash and pinched muscles in my side, but it had the desired effect on my brain. By the time Saul yelled at me to stop, I looked around at the hole I had dug and smiled even though I didn't have the energy or the pain tolerance to pull myself out of the hole. Lucky me, Lindsey was there to help me. When she was finished pulling me out of the hole, she handed the tall man from the office a bill and laughed.

"I really thought he'd die," she said.

They both laughed again and disappeared into the office. Saul gave me a business card and shook my hand.

"Once in a while I need a man to dig a hole on short notice. You're a good man. Call me if you'd like a job."

I nodded and went back to the office to find Lindsey. The office was empty, so I walked out to the front gate of the cemetery, where Lindsey's cruiser was parked. She was in the driver's seat and she was still talking to the man from the office. They were still laughing. Posey wasn't in the car and that pissed me off even more than being the butt of Lindsey's jokes. I got in the car, twisting my face into the most disgusted look I could manage until we drove away.

"You were there before I finished the hole, weren't you?"

"You had a deal," she said. "I wasn't going to interfere with that."

"Where's Posey?"

"She's working something out. I thought it was like my thing, you know, like an assault—"

"You think those guys raped my wife?"

"Not now. I don't think so. She's hard to read and I'm no therapist, but I don't get any of those vibes. She just seems focused on whatever she's trying to do."

"She knows more about what Taylor's up to than she's telling us."

"Well, duh, but she's not going to crack so move along."

"I'm her husband. She should tell me."

"Like you're Ward Fucking Cleaver? She's no happy housewife, you know that, right?"

"I guess. But what about trust and support and—"

"This is her world, bucko. You're the one who needs to be doing the trusting and supporting. You tell her everything about how you write your little stories and file your sperm paperwork or whatever it is you do all day?"

Dammit.

"No, I guess not," I said. "Sometimes I think I'm probably just better off on my own. I'm not cut out for this relationship crap."

She fist bumped my hand and said, "None of us are. Now tell me this big news of yours."

I started with my visit to the clinic and finding Taylor's schedule in the system and later finding out that it must have been flagged for security and the university police to have found out about it so quickly. Then I told her about my friends on the unit thinking these guards sounded a lot like Taylor's sons who had been thrown out of the clinic for causing trouble.

"Sons," she said. "I didn't see that coming. That doesn't make any sense."

"Right? I guess I kind of assumed the reason he was so wacky about this sample was because it was his last chance at a son or some kind of legacy BS."

"Were they sure it was his family?"

"Like they asked for ID or something? I don't know. You don't think they are?"

"I'm not jumping to conclusions," she said. "It's a lead, nothing more. But it's a good one. Something we can work with."

"We should tell Posey."

"No. We very much should not tell Posey," Lindsey said.

"I should be with her. I should be helping her, not you."

"You're not helping either of us. You should be at work staying the hell out of our way like I asked you to in the first place."

I spun to look directly at her and had an uncomfortable urge to smack her. That diminished my anger a bit, but not enough to tone down my screaming.

"You're the one who brought me into this in the first place," I said. "You stopped me. You called in the favor. You're the one who dumped all of this fucking guilt on me and pitted me against my wife and her brother and now you have the balls to tell me I'm not helping?"

I expected her to slam on the brakes and turn and give me some kind of lecture, but she kept driving and ignored me.

Being the savvy communicator I am, I pushed.

"My life, my wife's life, my unborn baby's life are all in peril now because you pulled me into your car and told me to go to work and be a good employee."

"Silly me," she said after a long pause. "I had no idea being a good employee meant going behind my back to have two criminals do what I asked you to do."

"I..."

Dammit.

"I'm sorry," I said. "Shit. You're right."

"I need you. I wouldn't have come to you if I didn't think *you* specifically had something I needed."

"Because you're a hateful shrew who wanted to spite my wife and rub her nose in—"

"Because I was hoping you'd be able to bridge our differences," she said softly.

"Oh. Really? Cause I'm kind of crap at that kind of stuff."

"So I see now."

"Shit," I said. "Now I feel like a giant ass."

"This is getting sappy. Let's be quiet for a bit and let the moment pass and we can get back to fixing your colossal fuck-up."

• • •

LINDSEY DROPPED me off at my apartment to think about what I'd done while she went to her station to dig up the complaints on Taylor's family from the cancer center and see what she could put together about them and their connections to the corrections department. I was told three different times not to bug or pressure Posey and that it would probably be best if I shut myself in the bathroom and didn't have any contact with the outside world.

And I really tried.

I tried harder at that than I have any other thing in my life aside from staying married. At first it was easy. I was hungry so I made some pizza rolls and dug around in the cupboards until I found some of the sour cream and onion Pringles I like so much. There was cold PBR in the house and a marathon of *Two and a Half Men* on so I settled in and prepared to continue the purging of my mind that had begun during my grave-digging stint. In fact, if I had been a little more on the ball I could have avoided the whole situation to begin with.

The *Two and a Half Men* marathon had just moved into the episodes after Charlie dies and is replaced by Walden Schmidt. The early episodes are abysmal and provided a good opportunity to get up and use the bathroom. I was in our bedroom where the cable signal was better, the bed was more comfortable than our couch, and the bathroom was only a few steps away. I was halfway to the bathroom when I heard a knock on the front door.

Before I made it out of the bedroom to check on the door, it exploded open. I spun back around and ran to the closet where Posey kept a shotgun for home protection and grabbed it, checking first to make sure it was loaded with live shells instead of the bean bag riot loads that Posey usually left me with and then backing into the bathroom—leaving the door open—to wait and see if I'd die or not.

"We know you're here." I recognized the voice as the guard who shot both of the Carter brothers.

I wasn't going to fall for the trap. My plan was still to avoid contact if I could and stay the hell out of the way. But one of them stepped into my bedroom and pointed a gun at me and I shot him. My aim, still so very miserable, missed the guy in front of me completely and nicked his partner/brother in the leg enough to drop him to the ground screaming. That still left the man in front of me fully capable of shooting me, which he did.

With a Taser.

In the balls.

I don't know if I blacked out from the blast of electricity or from the pain. But when I opened my eyes again I was tied to a chair in a basement somewhere that smelled like wet cat poop.

"We have a communication problem here," the man standing in front of me said. "You were going to tell your wife and your friend how serious we were about getting that sample and then they were going to get it for us."

As far as I knew, Titus never had cats, but as I looked around the basement, I recognized the two large deep freezers and the boxing bag hanging from the ceiling as his but the whole place smelled like wet cat poop. I assumed stray cats from the neighborhood had made their home down here and would probably be the last living things I had contact with before I died. My head was still mushy inside and to help focus my attention and my meager survival instincts, I focused on the details of the basement.

Titus wasn't the sort of guy who would have an elaborate man cave, but there was a ratty yellow sofa in the corner to my left that Posey and I had fooled around on once and an old-school projection TV with a VCR on top. There was also a small refrigerator next to the couch that had been converted to a beer tap for a full keg inside. I tried to imagine a scenario where any of these things could help me escape but nothing materialized. So I kept talking.

"I told them," I said.

He smacked me in the face. It was hard enough and embarrassing enough to be more painful than a punch. It was demeaning in a way that punching me wasn't. I struggled against my restraints to show my displeasure.

"You're going to get another chance," he said. "With some conditions."

"What's so important about that sample?"

He slapped me again.

"We did some digging around," he said. "Because I wanted to make sure before I killed you that I knew for sure if you were fucking with me or not."

I nodded and then shook my head no. The smacks and the electricity had scrambled me more than usual.

"I don't think the sample we want ever left the lab."

I straightened up and smiled.

"So we're good then?" I asked.

"Afraid not. I'm a bit embarrassed at how quickly I disposed of those other fellows, they could have been an asset."

"How do I know you won't accidentally kill me?"

He pointed to my balls.

"More Tasers," he said. "Fewer bullets. Improved margin of error."

I shook my head. It didn't stop shaking until several minutes after he stopped talking.

"So I'm going back in for the sample?" I asked.

"Easy in, easy out."

"At the risk of making myself expendable," I said, "what do you need me for?"

"You're the solution to a problem you created."

"You can't go back to the hospital because I called you out?"

He nodded.

"Well, I can't go back in for the same reason," I said.

He pointed his gun at my head.

"I guess we don't need you then."

"No. Wait," I said. "I know people. I'll find a way in. As long as I don't have to use a computer I should be fine."

He lowered the gun and his mouth twitched in one corner in what might have been an attempt at a smile. I pointed to his brother (though I still had doubts they were related to each other, let alone Morton Taylor) and his leg where I had shot him.

"I don't want him to die and me to get saddled with a murder rap," I said.

"I'll worry about him. You get our sample and everything will work out just fine."

"You're not wearing your prison guard uniforms," I said, despite yelling at my brain internally to shut up. "Are you two even related?"

He Tasered me again in the chest and when I came to the next time the guards were gone and I was free. Who were these guys? I really hoped Lindsey would have some luck digging through the cancer center complaints and finding a clue to who these assholes were. In the meantime, I had to find a way back to the hospital. Again. I still had the card for the cab company and the money Posey gave me last time, so this turned out to be one of the easier return trips.

My one chance at success with this hinged on a cancer center accountant named Delilah Dawson. She was a first line reconciler for all of the grant and development funds in the department. We had a workable relationship based on a shared interest in *Star Wars* and a shared distaste for office small talk. She spent her days buried in paperwork made up of real, live paper surrounded by real, live books and manuals and had one of the last three remaining typewriters in the entire health system in her office. This woman didn't like technology or people so she would be the last person to be aware that 1) I was no longer with the department and 2) I was wanted by the university police. She would also be able to help me find the paper backup ID system that was federally mandated for the samples and avoid me needing to touch a computer at all.

Her office was in a triangle-shaped building that had last been updated and relevant in the late 1970s. It had hallways that ended randomly and elevators that traveled to half floors and even an active file room in one of the ceilings. It also had secret passages. All of this was cool the first time I heard about it but quickly pissed me off when I had to navigate it quickly to find someone I was looking for. Delilah had told me once that she'd been offered the chance to move to the main hospital building with the rest of the department, but this bizarre building with poor phone service and no discernible Wi-Fi signal offered her the silence and protection from intrusion she craved. It took me an hour to find her office and I started on the same floor of the same building she was in. I'd say she was thoroughly protected from drop-ins. She was carefully dusting an Ewok bobblehead when I knocked on her door frame.

"Mr. Prince."

I bypassed small talk and dove right into what I needed her for.

"I have a patient *very* concerned about his specimen being tracked digitally so—"

"I'll get the tracking binder then we'll go," she said.

I followed her back up to the surface, trying to keep myself along the edge of the walls and in the shadows and out of sight lines as much as possible. Delilah was laser-focused on her forward progress and didn't seem at all worried or curious about my scattered travel pattern. I had a moment of panic when we emerged from the stairwell into the hallway and I came face-to-face with a campus police officer.

Expecting to immediately be grabbed and taken into custody, I stopped moving and let Delilah go on without me. But the guard just stepped out of the way and gave me a bit of a glare but nothing more sinister and went on his way. I had assumed I was some sort of high-priority campus-wide fugitive, but it appeared that wasn't the case. I was simultaneously relieved and disappointed. It's nice to be a big deal even if it's for the wrong reasons.

"Patient name," Delilah said when I found her.

"Morton Taylor."

"Junior or Senior?"

"Senior," I said, without realizing the immediate impact of the question.

"It's been removed. Three days ago."

That would have been the day I was sick and the Carter brothers raided the lab.

But wait a second.

"What about junior?"

She read off a string of letters and numbers I recognized as a sample serial number. Holy shit. *That* was the money sample but the brothers didn't know it. This wasn't about a childless gangster protecting his legacy and his only shot at a child, it was about protecting the offspring of his own insane and murderous offspring. And I needed to get it into the right hands.

"Is there a Titus Wade in there?"

She read off another string of numbers. I had both of the money samples at my fingertips. I was back to being someone important. I had the power. And I was going to use it to make things right. Delilah wrote out the numbers I needed on a Post-it note and retreated back to her Luddite lair. I wasn't ever going to get a better shot at the samples and I needed to get them out of the lab. I looked around everywhere I could for a couple of the liquid nitrogen vapor tanks that the department used for transporting the samples but couldn't find any.

And then I remembered one of the last tasks I'd actually accomplished at work before going down this warped rabbit hole had been to order more because there had only been one left. That's why they had been only limited to getting one sample out of the lab. It wasn't that they'd been surprised by an attack or by police, they just didn't know any other way to transport the samples except in the big white tanks everyone in the department knew about, even temporary janitors.

But I had been bored at my job and taken the seminar on emergency dry ice packing when it was offered. It only provided twenty-four hours of protection for the sample as opposed to the seven days that the liquid nitrogen tubes offered, but I had to take what I was given. I used the numbers Delilah left for me to find the storage canisters for the samples I was looking for and carefully packed them in a plastic cassette that would hold them in place and then buried them in the gel box that held the dry ice. I put the gel box into a foam box and put that into a specially fitted UPS box that I addressed to Posey's office with the departmental charge code and set it for early AM delivery.

I made a duplicate set-up with two other random samples but didn't put the second set into a UPS box. The last step was to put the foam box in a spare backpack that was lying around the lab and pretend I didn't know what I was carrying around on my back and dropping the other box into the UPS mail slot next to my desk. It was the last stop on the university driver's route and would make it to Posey's office by ten a.m. the next day. That would cut the active time I had with the samples to less than twelve hours but it would make sure that when—

"You're not trying to escape, are you?"

I looked up and saw my friends from corrections at the end of the hallway dressed in their uniforms once again and was happy I had risked the shortened time frame with the samples to make sure I wasn't holding them when the guards found me.

"Just trying to find a way out of here that won't get me killed," I said.

The guard who always talked pointed to my backpack.

"That our stuff?"

I nodded and dropped the backpack on the floor and kicked it toward them.

"Check it out if you want."

He picked up the pack and walked away.

"We've found you every time we need to, we'll find you if you've screwed us over."

I had no doubt of that, but hoped to have a plan in place long before they found out. My gut sense was that they wouldn't risk compromising the sample by opening it before they gave it to Taylor, but even if they did they'd see a very convincing pack job with actual samples they would have no way of knowing weren't the ones they wanted. That wouldn't be until Morton Taylor got the samples and checked them against his own records. If I didn't have my shit sorted out by that time, I was going to be in trouble deeper than just with Morton Taylor and his goons.

Once I was free of the lunatic guards, I was briefly tempted to go back for the UPS box. I had more flexibility with the time frame, but I needed to get a bunch of things lined up before the samples would come into play anyway. This way they were as safe as I could assure them to be and could track them if needed. I needed to regroup with Posey and Lindsey, but again, neither of them would answer their phones. I didn't want to just sit around waiting for them to find me. I needed more emotional insight and having seen the benefit even a short visit to my parents' house had given me, I needed another field visit. I was deciding between heading down to Toledo where Titus Wade had died or out to his old house when someone finally called me back.

"Valium," Parker said, "is apparently not the best thing to have coursing through your veins when you exit the hospital."

"They're letting you out? What was wrong?"

"Immediately what's wrong is my lack of wings," he said.

And then I knew I wanted to visit Titus Wade's house with a doped up Parker Farmington to hopefully bring this weird loop to a close. My Zipcar was still in the valet lot by the ER where I had left it after bringing Posey in from the trunk of her car. I'd been worried about picking it up at the time because of my run-in with the campus police. But now that I realized I wasn't campus villain #1, I felt more confident picking it up without fear of getting arrested. I'll admit that the five or six minutes it took them to bring me the car were tense, and at one point I almost ran when two campus police cruisers pulled up in front of me, but my car pulled up right behind them and in no time I was meeting Parker and a nurse on the other side of the hospital in the patient pickup area.

The nurse gave me a rundown of Parker's exit orders, helped me load him into my car, then left us alone. His attack had been nothing more than a nasty asthma attack triggered by any number of chemicals in the basement area where we'd been skulking around. The Valium responsible for his current loopy state was from a panic attack brought on by a poorly executed chest CT exam. And now I was going to take him out to the emotionally volatile Wade house. I was aware of being an awful person, but not aware enough to have any desire to change my course of action.

We'd been on the road for about ten minutes when I told Parker, "I got a call about *our book* while you were in the hospital."

"Yeah. About that. Sorry I didn't tell you. I never know how serious that guy is about anything."

"Ellis?"

Parker shook his head.

"He has this idea of teaming up with the university press to do separate versions of your book and mine so he can try to recoup some of his losses."

"Really," I said. "Print."

Call me old-fashioned or out of touch or just plain weird, but I needed a print book deal for it to feel real. To see my book on a bookstore shelf, even if I was the one who placed it there. To know that a physical object with words I wrote and a story I imagined would exist long after me. I might not have been destined for fame or accolades in my own time, but having a book in print bought me a lottery ticket for the bigger literary jackpot: immortality.

Parker waved his hands back and forth across his lap then snapped them into the air.

"They'll never go for it though," he said. "Too gross. Too gimmicky."

"You're not going to believe this," I said. "But I might have a pretty wicked marketing plan."

I explained what I had learned about the various samples and the familial history of our gangster patient.

"You can't add semen to ink," Parker said.

"That's not what I meant, but maybe now isn't the best time to talk about this."

"We'll regroup when I'm off these pills."

"Something like that, yes. For now, I'm taking you to Titus Wade's house to help me achieve some emotional closure."

"Because you're an ass?"

"Yes."

He grunted and fell asleep. My car was in the driveway of the house when I pulled up and I assumed Posey was there either plotting something or trying to get the same kind of closure I was. I thought about bringing Parker in with me to try and break the ice with Posey, but he looked so peaceful and another person probably wasn't going to do anything to make the situation less contentious, so I locked him in the car, leaving the windows open a bit, and left him in the driveway. We were out of the city limits in the more stable and reasonably safer area of Dearborn Heights.

The house was a two-bedroom bungalow on a street mostly made up of old people who were the original, mildly racist owners of the houses. I wondered if the street full of retired auto workers, teachers, and janitors knew they had a violent bounty hunter on their block. I also wondered what kind of neighbor Titus Wade had been. Had he hidden his violent side with block barbeques and candy for the neighbor kids, or was he that guy who complained about neighbors who didn't mow their lawns to his liking and waved his gun at anyone who ran the stop sign in front of his house.

Posey was in the kitchen sitting at the table eating from a White Castle crave case and drinking from a Diet Coke tall boy instead of her preferred Miller Lite when I found her. She waved me over and I sat down across from her and took two of the burgers from the case. I pulled the pickles off and offered them to her and she took them with a smile.

"There's a White Castle that Titus and I went to once in New Jersey and they had the worst pickles I've ever tasted," she said. "Like little green feet."

"Everything in New Jersey smells and tastes like feet," I said, having never been to New Jersey, but suspecting it was true based on everything I'd heard about it from television.

She smiled again, widely and effortlessly, then just as quickly tightened her lips and looked away from me.

"It's not what you think," she said.

I shrugged.

"We've never had a chatty relationship," I said. "I like it that way. I like that I can be inside my head and you can be inside yours and we don't have to bullshit about it."

She ate both of the pickles in one quick bite and wiped her fingers on her black yoga pants. I stared at her and marveled at the transition she'd made from flaky and temperamental creative writing student to flaky and temperamental, but professional and respected, bail bondsman. It was fun in my own head to think of her as a bounty hunter chasing down bad guys, but her business was mostly paperwork and road work to the local jails and courthouses. She did have to track down people once in a while, but they were very rarely really bad guys and she did most of her tracking with her phone and her laptop. It's why I hadn't really worried about her keeping up her work schedule during the early months of her pregnancy.

Then I found her in the trunk of her own burning car.

"Nobody put me in there," she said. "I had a flat tire in the wrong place at the wrong time. I was leaning in for the jack and—"

"I love that we don't need to talk things out. We don't need to play games or bullshit each other or listen to whatever inane shit is going through the other person's head."

"There was some sort of riot going on at the liquor store and I didn't want to wait for—"

"I really don't need to know," I said. "I see your face, there's no panic in telling the story, your body language is relaxed, but even if you were jittery as all hell, it wouldn't matter. I trust you. You tell me what you need to tell me."

She nodded and ate another burger.

"But when I start to get nervous, when this doesn't work for me anymore," I continued, "is when you're not around."

I took another burger this time, mostly to stop myself from saying anything else. It was true that we didn't have a chatty relationship, and it was true that I was okay with that, but it was also true that once I *did* start talking to her, or anyone for that matter, it was very hard for me to stop. I almost always ended up saying something I regretted. I didn't want to regret anything I said to Posey right then.

And I didn't have to. She put her hand on mine and brushed her leg against mine. I expected her to say something else, but in light of the current conversation it made sense that we'd make more of a connection non-verbally. She smiled again and I lost my breath for a quick second. I'd seen her smile more in that ten minutes in her dead brother's house than I had in the almost a week I'd been fooling around with these stupid sperm samples. And it was always her smile that did it for me.

She'd changed her look, parts of her personality, her career, and her outlook on life since I'd known her, but her smile was the consistent marker for my feelings. It was what I looked for when I came home after a shitty day at work or a good day at work. It was what drove me to try better, to do better, to aim better. And in bed, it was what I worked for. She could fake other things, but she couldn't fake that smile.

"I'm here now," she said.

She took my hand and led me back to the smaller of the bedrooms. It was paneled like a northern Michigan hunting cabin and the twin bed had a quilt on it that made me think of winter despite the heat outside. We stood in front of the bed and I ran my hands through her hair and across her face and I kissed her quickly on the lips and then around her neck and then a deeper kiss while I ran my hands across her slight baby bump before gently pushing her back onto the bed.

I've never liked making out. I like kissing, I even like tongue kissing, but I prefer it in small doses and I get bored with it very quickly. Part of it has always been my bad sinuses and I have a hard time breathing if the kissing goes on for too long. The other reason is Posey tended to take making out waaaaay too seriously. Instead of the smiles I craved, I got melodramatic eye rolls and deep breathing that made me giggle inappropriately and made her mad at me. I also found, with Posey at least, there were other parts of her I enjoyed kissing much more.

I flopped on to the bed next to her and unbuttoned her pants.

"You're sure I'm not going to poke its head if I get too far up there?"

"That's not funny," she said and I immediately feared I'd blown my traditional first move, which was always a cheesy joke to break the tension. "It's also not true. At this point we've been away from this long enough you should worry more about bats up there."

She smiled and we were off.

• • •

AFTERWARD, I knew better than to break the spell with a joke. She had her head on my chest and we were basking in the glow of the moment and the cool breeze of the air conditioner blowing through the room. The mental clock in my head for the health of the samples was ticking, but in Titus Wade's house with his naked pregnant sister curled around me seemed like a spectacularly bad time to bring up his frozen sperm. I also thought about asking if she'd heard from Lindsey but that didn't seem like any better of an idea, so I kept my mouth shut, talked myself out of any number of dumb ideas in my head, and every once in a while even managed to enjoy the moment. We fell asleep for about an hour and then the issue of what to do with the samples and with Lindsey banged on the door.

Posey startled herself awake and between the disorientation of being woken up in the middle of sleep and the complexities of getting her awkwardly shaped body off of me and out of bed it took a while for me to get to the door, where I found Lindsey crying and bloodied. She pushed past me and went to Posey. I followed and instead of seeing Posey hiding herself with the sheet or scrambling to get back into her clothes she was standing fully nude and hugging Lindsey with a friendly intimacy I wasn't comfortable with. I had no fear that she was cheating on me with Lindsey, I was more worried about them scheming without me. I'd already felt close to being written out of this story a few other times. I would hate to find out it had already happened and I'd been narrating the wrong story the whole time.

It could also be that pregnancy had shattered the discomfort Posey had with nudity that hampered our early attempts at sexual compatibility. I hoped it was the second but wondered if I should plan for the first.

I was relegated to the kitchen to guard the hamburgers while Posey and Lindsey talked amongst themselves. When they finally emerged, both fully clothed, Lindsey sat down where I had been sitting earlier and took two burgers and removed the pickles before scarfing them, and six more, down. She offered me the sixteen discarded pickles on a napkin and I waved her off with a smirk.

"They assaulted her," Posey said. "And we've been deputized for revenge."

I didn't need to ask if she was talking about the guards and I didn't need to be briefed that *assault* was a conversational way of saying they'd raped her. The revenge part, though, was stumping me.

"Shouldn't we call the police?" I asked.

"Fucking police," Lindsey said. "Let me tell you about the fucking police after fucking…fucking."

"We're going to Morton Taylor," Posey interjected, "and

exchange his sample for his help setting these two assholes up."

"The looks those fucking cops gave me," Lindsey continued. "Like it was my fault."

I wasn't sure if she was talking about her current assault or the one from her past that inspired her toward a monogamy pact with god that was at the center of her pursuit of Titus's final gift. Either way I had nothing to add so I nodded while she kept talking.

"Woulda been their call I'da been out on my ass and lost my pension and my seniority just so they didn't have to look at me and maybe think about what happened to me and maybe, god forbid, sympathize with me."

Another burger, another discarded pickle.

"But I showed them. Bet you didn't know I'm still technically DPS. Got me one of them fancy civil rights lawyers and beat 'em until they transferred me to the university. Better pay, better hours, better everything."

"And they can't fire you for taking the heat when a campus professor and student kill a serial killer and a bounty hunter whose bodies are never found," I said.

She pointed at me with her fingers in a gun shape and winked at me.

"Exactly."

"So these guards, we're just going to set them up and kill them? Flat out? No—"

"We're going to help a friend," Posey said. "Nobody said anything about killing anyone."

"When did you two become friends?"

Posey moved behind me and put her arms around my neck.

"You assumed we hate each other," she said. "You project

your simplistic view of this world onto us and don't bother exploring the full complexity of the issues or the participants."

"She was the one going behind your back with this whole thing, trying to use me to get what you wanted," I said.

Lindsey had moved away from the table and was scrounging through the refrigerator. She turned around when she found another tall boy.

"If I'da told you," Lindsey said, opening the beer, "that I ran the whole idea by her first and she thought it was a good idea for you to help me out, would you have been as eager to help?"

My brain was seizing with panic and confusion. This couldn't be right. They were setting me up. I ran all of my recent interactions with them through my head looking for clues but I was seeing it through the haze of self-justification and didn't know how much of it I could trust.

Posey massaged my shoulders and said, "I keep trying to tell you everything isn't about you. I don't say it to be mean but to avoid situations like this where your…focus…can affect other people."

Lindsey was pacing around the kitchen, sitting briefly at the table, and then going to the fridge and then walking to the back door and then sitting back down.

"Look at her," I said. "My *focus* aside, any plan we go in with that involves her will end in death."

"Then stay in your fucking hole and forget what you owe me and your pregnant wife and I will take care of this problem too."

"Too?" I asked. "What in the hell is that supposed to mean?"

"Let it go, baby," Posey said. "Just get us the sample and

you can get back to work on your new book and we'll—"

I pushed her hands off of me and stood up.

"I can't go back. I already tried to help, probably due to some kind of narcissistic focus problem, and got myself locked out of their computer system and on a security watch list."

"Jesus Christ," Lindsey said.

She took a deep breath and sat down next to me. Then she punched me. She hit me twice in the chest and knocked me out of my chair then fell down next to me. Posey tried to help me up but Lindsey pushed her away. She rolled on top of me and kissed me.

"I've had enough violation in my life," she said. "It's time for me to take what I—"

Posey pulled her off of me before that weird scenario could develop any further. I scurried to the furthest corner of the kitchen before trying to stand up on my own. As I watched Posey help Lindsey up as well, I knew I had to do something to maintain my leverage and my involvement.

"We're not going to Morton Taylor," I said. "We're going directly to the guards."

Posey propped Lindsey up in one of the kitchen chairs then side-eyed me with a pleading glance.

"Not now, Dominick. We'll work this out later."

"Any scenario through Morton Taylor gives him and the guards the leverage. They killed the Carter brothers. They attacked Lindsey. They…who knows what they've done to you. But they haven't—"

"I told you nothing happened."

"They've had the chance to kill me twice and let me go so I could get the samples. We've got the leverage. *I've* got the leverage."

"You've got bullshit," Lindsey snarled.

"You're right. I've got nothing," I said. "I'll go home and wait like a puppy dog for my wife and her friend to come home."

I started to leave; I wanted to leave. I wanted more perfect parting words and the moral authority. But I was on a roll and I was too far away from the Crave Case to keep my mouth shut with food. So I turned back toward them and kept talking.

"But you won't come home. Because you didn't listen to me. You're going to plot some crap ass scheme to the best of your knowledge but it's going to fail and you're going to be murdered and I'm going to have to live with that. Because this is *my* story. I'm the hero. I'm not expendable. And the sooner you two realize that the sooner we can get to work really fixing this."

"We'll talk at home later, baby," Posey said.

"Shit, no, he's right," Lindsey said. "Goddammit, he's right. They won't kill him. Not right away. Sexist assholes."

"But you said you can't go back to the hospital," Posey said. "How are we going to get the samples?"

Brief pause. Make them think they've found a way to write me out of the story again and then:

"I already got the samples out," I said. "Before I came over here. Shit. Parker's still out in the car."

"He's got the samples? How did you get them out? How long are they good for?"

Now it was my turn to put my arms around Posey and calm her down. I massaged her shoulders and explained what I had done.

"I have to be the one to sign for them or the driver won't leave the package," I said. "We've got about twelve hours to get a plan together."

"Man," Posey said. "That's a tight window."

I pointed over to Lindsey.

"What would really help is if she was able to find out anything good in those complaints against these guys."

"Well, let me tell you about that," Lindsey said.

And then she passed out.

I went out to the car and shook Parker awake and told him what was going on and asked him if he could return my car for me.

"I thought you needed me for an emotional breakthrough or something."

"Plans changed," I said.

"What hasn't changed," he said slowly, "is the fact that I just got out of the hospital and I am not allowed to drive while heavily medicated."

"Shit. Right. Well, come on in then. You could probably use some food then. Lindsey just passed out so you can eat her food."

Back inside, we moved the food to the living room and sat around staring at each other trying to figure out the best way to do this without anyone dying.

"I really think we're overcomplicating this," I said. "I've got what they want. There's only two of them and they travel together. We give them a time and a place for the meeting and grab them when they show up."

"Grab them and do what?" Posey asked.

"Give them to the cops. I'm an eyewitness to them murdering

two people and Lindsey can file against them for her attack."

"You heard Lindsey, the cops will never believe her over two of their own and you didn't report the murder right away, which makes you look guilty as hell. That's a lot of doubt and if the cops don't lock these guys up immediately they'll hunt us down and kill us."

I nodded and leaned back in my chair. As much as I fancied myself a leader or the smart guy in the room, I was better at shouting out ideas and waiting for someone smarter to filter out the crap and find the good in whatever I said.

We stared at each other some more, waiting for inspiration and working through the rest of the food in the house.

"The office is wired for video and sound," I said. "What if we can get them to confess?"

Posey thought about that for a bit, nodding.

"It's not a bad idea, but video can be edited and tampered with. We'd have to have the cops watching the feed and I don't know that anyone would be willing to do that for us."

More nodding. When all of the food was gone I said, "There's really only one way this is going to work. We need to get them to kill each other."

The idea, even upon further reflection, seemed like a good one. We were still at a loss though on how to best execute it. If we had more time, we would try to split them up and turn them against each other. But the clock was ticking and we didn't even know their names, let alone enough about them to spot weaknesses and exploit them. Posey was suspiciously quiet during the discussions and Lindsey was still groggy so her input was minimal at best.

When we finally got sick of staring at each other without making any further progress, we all agreed to disband to our separate areas and reconvene early the next morning and see if anything came to us overnight. Lindsey agreed to drop off Parker; I assumed she needed whatever weird comfort Parker provided her to work through the repercussions of her attack. I was heading to my car when Posey waved me back into the house.

"I'm staying here tonight," she said.

I nodded again, hyperaware of trying to maintain the silent, comfortable relationship I had babbled on about to her earlier. She seemed like she wanted to talk though so I followed her back into the living room and sat down next to her on the couch. The TV was off and the only sound was the loud hum of the window air conditioner keeping us from boiling in our own body juices.

"So, Lindsey and Parker," I said. "Whoa, right?"

"I told you they didn't do anything to me and that's true but it's not exactly the whole story."

"Oh," I said. "Do we need to get more food?"

"I introduced you to Rickard and you never asked any questions about our history together or how I knew him. I've always appreciated that."

"Okay…"

"I don't know if those guys are really corrections officers, I suspect they are, but maybe not really assigned to Mort because that would violate *so* many different rules."

I tried not to notice the overly casual way she referred to him as Mort.

"But I do know," she continued, "that they are brothers, stepbrothers actually, and the one thing that could break them up is me."

"Oh," I said again, with even less feigned enthusiasm.

"It's not what you think. It's not sex. It's about Rickard. How I encouraged him and…well, the one who always talks, his name is Charlie, and he's a grade A textbook definition asshole and he thinks I brainwashed his kid brother."

"Okay."

What else really was there to say?

"And I guess I did. I tried to break him free, get him to see the world beyond his fucked up family, and he did."

"And became a serial killer."

"The other one, Jay, he's the quiet one but he's in tight with his dad. He's the appointed heir of the tiny backwoods crime empire these morons run. Or at least he was until Rickard—"

"Where did that name even come from?" I asked. "Are you the only one who called him that?"

"It was part of the breaking free. He didn't want his father's name influencing his future. We found the name in a bookstore and he liked it."

"It sounds like both of these guys hated you equally."

"But they disagree about what to do with me. Jay wants to ruin me and ruin my business and run me out of town."

"Ugh," I said. "That sounds—"

"Jay wants to kill me."

"Oh."

Again with the brilliant wordsmithing on my part.

"And this is where it gets complicated for us," she said. "This is why I haven't been around much. I've been out trying to find a way around this, around you having to deal with this."

"Because I can't protect you like I should? I'm not man enough? I'm not—"

"You're not the father."

"I...I don't even..."

"Whatever sample you have isn't the only one."

Fuck. Fuck. FUCK.

I wanted to smack her. I wanted to hug her. I wanted to strangle her. But I put my hand on her belly instead. She sucked in a panicked breath when I came at her and her body language remained tense as I moved it around.

"So you…I mean, was it artificial or…"

I tried to backdate our relationship and the last time she'd seen Rickard and when she found out she was pregnant and couldn't make any of it work.

"Yes, it was artificial," she said.

"Why? After everything you saw and everything you knew?"

"You have no idea what I saw or what I knew, Dominick. This was my insurance policy."

"What about us?"

"I know this isn't what you had in mind. I know how you felt about him."

"You lied to me."

She nodded.

I let out a long sigh and was surprised to find myself calm and free of vomit. But I wanted to kill everybody. I wanted a blazing gunfight that took out everyone. Including me. There was nothing to save, nothing to protect. Only rage.

"We take care of this," I said. "And then we're done."

She nodded again.

Driving back to my apartment downtown, likely for the last time, I tried not to think. How much did Lindsey know? Parker? Did Big Mort and his stepsons know all of this? Was that the insurance? Or was Posey planning on dropping it at the meeting? Did it matter? It wouldn't change my planning. I wanted everyone in the same room, open the samples, let the revelations fly, and see who survived and go from there. Like the end of an old British mystery only with more guns.

I stopped off at the apartment, made a sappy and sentimental round where I touched the walls and allowed myself a few moments of grief, and then moved to the bedroom, where I packed as much of my stuff as I could into suitcases and grabbed the shotgun and all of the shells I could find and had my hand on the doorknob for more than five minutes before I went back into the bedroom and flopped on the bed.

My over-analytical nature took over and I was swept over by the full rush of every thought I'd been pushing away. I wallowed in what my future would look like and let myself imagine every worst-case scenario, including my own death and that of Posey and the baby. After a brief break to dig through the kitchen and find the strongest alcohol we had, I sunk back onto the bed and drank and cried until I passed out. When my eyes opened again it was 12:30 the next afternoon.

• • •

I HAD voicemail messages on my phone from Posey and Lindsey that only told me to call them back as soon as I could, with no useful information. Though I suppose given the time of day that was all the information I needed. My head was still spinning from the alcohol and the secrets so when I stood up I thought I was going to throw up. When I didn't, I briefly marveled at the irony of how many times I had puked in less toxic and less alcoholic-soaked situations but here I was wasted and crushed and couldn't vomit if my life depended on it. Lucky for me, I didn't much care for my life right then and had no illusions of saving it.

But I needed to put on the appearance of caring and that meant sustenance. Another forage through the kitchen netted me a warm Gatorade and a recently expired energy bar. I capped the meal off with a banana, initially unsure how my body would handle this rare influx of fruit, but it made a surprising difference in my mood and my energy level so I had another one then headed over to Posey's office.

The door was open and I heard yelling when I walked in and briefly thought about walking away. I was sure the UPS driver had left a contact tag and someone in there was smart enough to figure out a way around the signature requirement I'd put on it. So I wasn't integral to the scene, despite trying to force my way in at every turn. But that's not who I am. I'm too stubborn; too nosy, too self-centered to believe that any situation couldn't be made better by my involvement. Lindsey, Parker, and Posey were clustered around her desk and I walked in just in time to see Posey clock Parker right across the face.

I knew that punch was a long time coming and was seeded deep in the relationship they had going before I popped into their lives, but it still shocked me to see it. I was less shocked to see Parker swing wildly and try to hit her back. Lindsey blocked the punch though and pushed him to the ground as I cleared my throat.

"I take it you told them?"

"Not now, Dominick," Posey said, helping Parker to his feet.

Lindsey held up a brown sticker and cleared her own throat, mocking me.

"Tell us about this," she said.

"I expected to be here when it was delivered."

"But you were delayed. How convenient."

"We've got ten hours before the samples are compromised,"

I said. "We need a plan first."

Lindsey waved her arm disingenuously toward Posey.

"She seems to think she can turn these nut jobs against each other and get them to kill each other."

"I think she's right," I said. "But we should have some kind of backup plan just in case."

"I brought a shotgun," Posey said. "There's a handgun in the drawer there and one in the can under the sink."

I sighed again. It was turning into my default response and seemed to work better for me than just screaming every time I heard any of these people in my life say something. Maybe I needed to get some noise-canceling headphones. Or maybe I just needed to get a new life.

"So it really is going to come to killing them?" I asked.

"Not if we don't have to," Posey said. "But you're talking alternate plans. That means the ideal scenario failed."

"The ideal scenario," I said. "Where they kill each other."

"Don't be a naïve dumbass," Lindsey said. "They were always going to end up dead."

I thought back briefly to all of the PI novels I read and loved where the upstanding white knight PI took on the case of extracting a female client from some kind of trouble they were in with a gangster or other bad element. The PI would always set up some kind of swap or standoff with every intention of it going according to plan and everyone leaving on good terms and alive. Except he'd always bring along his gun-toting psycho sidekick as well, just in case, and it always ended with the sidekick blowing away all of the bad guys, solving the problem and leaving the PI with a mostly clean conscience. I couldn't figure out if I was the white knight or the psycho sidekick, but I still wasn't comfortable with it either way.

Parker broke my train of thought when he staggered around the desk and slammed into the wall. I remembered it hadn't been that long since he'd been in a hospital bed. I still didn't quite buy the chemical asthma attack nonsense they'd given me. I suspected it had more to do with what he found himself in the middle of: more of a panic attack sort of scenario. He'd gone from the villain of my previous narrative to my savior, briefly, to the only person whose well-being I was concerned with currently. I found a bottle of water in the small office fridge and handed it over to him.

"Should you even be here?" I asked. "Considering it's been less than—"

"He's here for me," Lindsey said. "For support."

I looked over at Posey when Lindsey said that, hoping for some kind of look or crack of a smile or anything that would indicate we'd be okay, but I got nothing but a hard stare. I knew this had to be hard on her. Despite my self-centered nature and notorious lack of concern for the well-being of others, I am capable of empathy and I tried to think about how I would act in the same scenario. But all that did was raise a bunch of questions I couldn't answer. So I pushed forward with blind optimism that everything would work out swell and I'd find a way to survive as I always had.

"Okay, then," I said, grabbing the UPS ticket from Lindsey. "I've had to do this a bunch of times before when packages were delivered at work and no one was there to pick it up. I just need to go to the website and type in this number and my account info and we can put in a different address for the package to go to, or we can have it delivered back here. I had it delivered here because it was the only address close by I could remember off the top of my head. But if anyone has a better idea, maybe part of a *plan*, perhaps, we could have it delivered there instead."

"Here," Posey said. "It's home turf."

"If you can change the location, can you change the signature?"

I looked over to Lindsey, who seemed to be deep in thought. Maybe she wasn't totally set on the "everyone must die" ending.

"I think so," I said. "I haven't done it before but I'm pretty sure it's an option."

She nodded.

"Then maybe," she said slowly, "we don't need to be here at all."

I liked the sound of that.

"Or," Posey said, "we bypass Mort's death squad, and go directly to him."

Lindsey frowned and squinted her eyes like she'd just found the source of a foul odor.

"This has gone beyond him," she said. "These guys are rogue. They've got murder on their minds and the only way we can get out of this for good is to deal with them."

"No, they still listen to him. You don't know this family. You don't know—"

"This isn't a family," Lindsey said. "It's a murder factory and going to the dying old head of this monster won't stop the rest of the body from killing us all before it dies."

The metaphors had grown pretty wild for my taste and I didn't like the renewed divide between Posey and Lindsey. As much as I distrusted their motives when they seemed like they were on the same side, I didn't feel in as much danger.

"I don't think we're going to settle this here," I said. "Or at all for that matter. Since nobody has one single plan that sounds viable, maybe we do both."

"In your long history of saying stupid shit," Lindsey said, "that might be the—"

"He's right," Parker said.

"You're woozy," Lindsey said. "Leave this to—"

Posey pointed to Lindsey and I thought they were finally going to punch it out, but she put her hand down and came over to stand next to me.

"Like he said, we've got time. You and Parker set up delivery of the package directly to the goons and Dominick and I will go and talk to Daddy. If we fail, you two are up and you can take out the boys."

Everyone nodded in agreement and we split up. Posey asked me to drive her car and I said yes even though I was shaking so hard I expected to rip the steering wheel off. I calmed myself down enough to get directions to the prison, but she put her hand on my leg and shook her head.

"We're not going to the prison," she said. "We're going to his house."

I followed her directions and was so proud of myself for staying quiet and not breaking the illusion of confidence I thought I had going. I'm sure she knew me well enough to see right through it, but I was looking for any small victory I could muster, even if it was only perceived. We headed out of the downtown area on I-94 heading north, and the grime of the city eventually gave way to the greenery of the outer city and then finally the manicured brick walls and planned communities of the wealthy suburbs. Posey had me exit at 11 Mile in St. Clair Shores and we headed toward the water and a few turns later we were pulling up to the circle drive of a gaudy stone mansion that backed up to prime waterfront property.

"I will talk," she said. "No matter what I say or what you hear: Just. Let. Me. Talk."

"That doesn't sound ominous at all," I said.

She huffed and got out of the car without saying anything else to me. I hung back, slightly behind her, as she rang the doorbell and chatted up the thick male nurse that answered the door. We were waved into the large open house quickly and led off to the east wing of the house where the shiny open spaces quickly became darker and more claustrophobic. The clean fresh smells of flowers and summer air were squelched by the antiseptic smells of a hospital. I tensed up and caught my breath when we entered and I saw two guards in dark gray corrections uniforms standing at the foot of Taylor's bed. But I kept quiet and quickly realized they were different guards and seemed lackadaisical at best about the number of Taylor goons milling about the room. Taylor strained to see who was invading his space and a wide smirk ran across his face when he saw Posey.

"The prodigal daughter returns," he said. "Going to try and kill me again?"

Posey snapped her head back to see how I was going to react to that. I was too stunned to say anything so I looked like I was doing a better job of following directions than I probably would have under different circumstances.

But man, my brain was getting whiplash from the revelations. It was like my life had suddenly turned into an English language telenovela.

"Morton," she said, coldly, "your fantasies are getting the better of you again, I see."

He groaned and waved her off.

"Better than the bullshit you keep trying to feed me."

She stepped closer toward the bed, but slower and more aware of the others in the room.

"Things have gone to shit quickly," she said, continuing her slow walk. "We need to have a talk."

"Talking is all we ever do but talking is what put me here.

Talking is what's killing me. Talking. Talking. Talking. What more is there to say?"

"Charlie and Jay have gotten out of hand. You're losing control of them and you're going to lose me," she said. "You're going to lose *us*."

I had no illusions that the us referred to her and me as opposed to her and the baby. But it was still hard to hear. I was confused and depressed, which was a horrible combination of emotions to be dealing with. I was still confused about what Taylor wanted from the sample. He already had kids so it wasn't his last ditch at offspring, and if he wanted to make sure his serial killer kid's offspring didn't see the light of day, then why would it matter if Posey died? She squatted down so she was at eye level with Taylor.

"You know this is the only way," she continued.

Taylor groaned and turned away from her.

"I don't like being pushed," he said. "This is blackmail."

"If it was blackmail you'd put a bullet in my head and be done with it. This is—"

"This is too much for an old man to deal with. That why I had the boys take care of it."

"They're blunt instruments. This is a delicate situation. If you and I don't work something out here, today, I'm going to give them what they've been looking for and they're going to kill me. They're going to die. Everyone is going to die and that will be your legacy."

Another groan, this one more resigned.

"I've already lost them," he said. "I couldn't stop them if I wanted to."

"Yes you can. But you don't want to."

"Never could bullshit you, could I? The truth though? I just don't fucking care anymore. I'll be gone and it was just the medicine and the stress of treatment…it messes with a man, a man like me who has always been too concerned with how I look to other people. Legacy. Such a stupid fucking word, a stupid fucking idea, like anyone running around with my last name is some kind of accessory to pass on like a pocket watch."

"Don't say that."

It was more of a desperate plea than a command. I didn't like at all how she sounded when she said it and I liked even less what it hinted her next move might be.

"Just get rid of it," he said. "You'll be taken care of."

I waited for some kind of verbal response from Posey but before I realized there wasn't going to be one, she already had her hands around his neck. She moved so quickly and so effortlessly that it went unnoticed by everyone else in the room as well, including the guards and Taylor's goons. Taylor wasn't going to go quietly though and quickly his gurgling and thrashing caught everyone's attention, including mine. I ran to Posey and tried to pull her off, but my minimal upper body strength was no match for her strength and training and blood lust.

The guards were less concerned with Posey's safety, though, and had their guns pulled and aimed before I could pull at her again. They screamed various versions of "stop and put your hands up," all of which she ignored while she continued strangling the life out of Morton Taylor. One of the guards fired and hit her in the arm, knocking her away from the bed. Taylor's goons took over from there and gunned down both of the guards.

I was briefly stunned at how many guns had made it into the home of a gangster under house arrest before my survival and protective instincts took over and I ran to cover Posey from any further gunfire. While her survival was certainly tied to my own survival, I was happy to find I still had strong feelings for her that included taking a bullet for her if necessary. Maybe I just didn't want to live with the guilt if she died and I didn't try to stop it. Likely it was somewhere between the two.

There were no more bullets, though, and she pushed me off of her and went right back to where she left off. This time her resolve was less enthusiastic and I was able to easily pull her back. One of the goons, a tall, gangly fellow with a faux hawk and a too trendy hipster suit, came over to us with a retro-looking revolver in one hand and a business card in the other. I dove at him, trying to knock him down or knock the gun away with spectacularly pathetic results.

"He was right," he said, handing Posey the card. "It's in his will. Nobody's allowed to touch you, but if you make the baby go away you get a nice chunk of change."

She took the card without a word and I followed her out to the car, still unsure what exactly had happened and who was going to be responsible for cleaning up the mess and whether or not cops would be showing up at my door to question and/or blame me for this. I also wondered if I even still had a door for them to show up at.

• • •

"So," I said when we had been driving long enough for me to think she might have calmed down a bit. "That didn't go very well at all."

"Pull over."

I was driving because she was using both of her hands to keep a tourniquet she'd made from her shirt tight on the gunshot wound in her arm. Her utilitarian black bra made me smile at her complete lack of vanity and seeing her pale white skin exposed triggered my husbandly protector instinct again

"We need to get you to the hospital."

"And tell them what? Is there a good way to explain this? Pull over."

I waited until there was a good-sized clearing on the side of the highway and pulled off. Posey got out of the car and at first I thought she was running away, but she banged on the trunk for me to open it. I popped the trunk with a button in the glove box and watched her in the rearview mirror as she pulled out an orange tackle box and got back in the car.

"I know you don't understand, Dom, but I really thought this was…this seemed like the only way to make it work."

"By strangling him?"

The tackle box was some kind of elaborate first aid kit and while she talked, she worked on her arm and cleaned it and bandaged it.

"I can't believe I was so wrong about him. About us."

"Where did you learn how to do that?" I asked, intrigued and sad that there was one more facet of my wife I had missed.

"YouTube mostly," she said. "And practice every once in a while when I have to shoot someone and I don't want them to die before I can get them to the court. This one isn't bad. Deep scratch kind of thing, no bullet lodged in the skin. Just want to make sure it stays clean and doesn't get infected."

"What is the deal with you and that family anyway?"

She cocked her head toward me and rolled her eyes as she tapped off the last of the bandage and closed the box.

"I thought you were comfortable not knowing the full details."

"You and I both know that was posturing bullshit and that I'm far too nosy and self-conscious not to want to know everything about it."

"Mmmm-hmmm."

"I get why he wants all the gooey evidence gone," I said. "What I don't understand is why you thought impregnating yourself with some of it would make any difference."

"I know he seemed insane and you only saw him as a murderer, but there was something amazing in there, something that could change the world, and he knew that."

"Rickard?"

She nodded.

"The guy who killed your brother?"

"What better way to show how committed I was to the idea? I just wanted him to see that if the genes were mixed right and the kid was raised right—"

"You'd raise a genius instead of a serial killer?"

She grabbed my hand and with one gesture and nine words broke my heart and my world.

"*We'd* raise a genius instead of a serial killer."

"You and me?"

"You'd be perfect for this, Dom. This is you. This is what you could become. What you could leave as your legacy."

My wife was insane. That was the only explanation. And I was insane for seeing her as sympathetic and possibly even right, rather than as a lunatic quickly unraveling. I pulled my hand away from hers and scooted away from her and closer to my door.

"I don't even know what to do with that. This is…back there you…I mean for god's sake. You strangled him to death?"

"You'd rather I shot him?"

I literally threw my hands in the air when she said that. There was nothing else I could do. My wife was going to kill everyone. Possibly even me.

"Let's just go home please," I said. "I can't do this anymore."

"No way," she said. "We're in this now. I'm not letting you run free so they can grab you and get the upper hand."

"I *don't* want any*thing* to do with this, Posey. I'm not joining your murder squad."

Posey sighed and I thought she was gearing up for another round of verbal justifications and bullshit theories, but instead she wiped her eyes with her fist and remained silent until we pulled back in front of the office. I parked the car out in front of the building in a no parking lane and watched Posey go inside. I stayed in the car, seeing no possible reason to follow her. I couldn't see a reason to leave either. Scenario after scenario ran through my head, from the inane to the sexist to the farthest fetched, and I couldn't come to any sort of rationale for what was going on. Well, none other than the obvious. She'd long tried to fight off the criminal and homicidal impulses of her brother. Maybe it was a deeper family thing and maybe she'd given up fighting it. I wanted to believe she was different but maybe she wasn't; maybe this was her.

Then what to do about it?

Dammit. She was right. I was in it. I could walk away all

I wanted but all that would do was leave me vulnerable. Was this an issue of sticking with the murderer I know opposed to the murderer I don't?

And the baby?

My baby?

Sort of. In my mind at least. I needed to protect them both.

Dammit.

I got out of the car and was walking toward the door when I saw three uniformed police officers coming my way. For a second I thought I could talk to them or go down to the police headquarters over by the casino and talk to a detective and explain everything and tell them what I saw and what I knew and get them involved to stop this before it got out of control. But it was already out of control and I knew it when I couldn't find a way to explain what was going on that didn't make me look like a criminal already. She was right. Right. Right. Right. I was stuck with them.

So the only thing to do was try to be the voice of reason.

Me. The voice. Of reason.

Fuck.

"Lindsey thinks we should go to the cops about this," Posey said, checking on the wound on her arm and changing the bandage.

I looked around for hidden cameras, finally convinced this was the most elaborate television prank in history. Lindsey was sitting behind Posey's desk scratching out notes or doodling or doing something with a legal pad in front of her. Parker was sitting in the client chair closest to me and he looked like every bit of energy he possessed was being used just to keep him upright.

"Your wife has a rotten sense of humor," Lindsey said. "The box is coming back here in about twenty minutes and we've contacted our friends to come and pick it up."

"And that's it then?" I asked. "They take what they want, they leave us alone, and we move on with our lives?"

Parker wobbled and I moved to grab him if he fell, but he stood up instead.

"We have an announcement," he said.

The way his words wobbled out of his mouth like he had wobbled out of his chair, I suspected he was drunk rather than sick. Or maybe he was both. I'd never known him to hold his liquor very well.

"Maybe this isn't the right time," Lindsey said, glaring at Parker. "And it's certainly not the right—"

"I had this little bottle of very expensive scotch I've been meaning to save for a very special occasion and this is definitely a *special* occasion," Parker continued. "But I don't have it with me so I found that bottle of whatever was in the drawer there—and I mean really, the hardboiled bail agent with the bottle of booze in the drawer, could you get any more cliché with that?"

"Is there a point to your—"

"We're having a baby," he said. And then he sat back down in the chair with no follow-up.

I stood in stunned silence. Posey had no use for silence, stunned or otherwise, and lit into both of them with a rant of gibberish and spittle that amused and frightened me.

"Yes," Lindsey said when Posey was done. "Surprise. But it's not what you think. It's not your brother's."

"Isn't that *great,*" Parker said. "She's transitioning from victim to survivor. Like an Oprah woman, or a Lifetime movie heroine."

"Congratulations," I finally said. "Though he seems to be kind of an asshole about it."

"We talked a lot while you two were gone—"

"And you haven't even asked about how that went," Posey yelled at kind of a ridiculously loud volume.

I'd seen drunk people and angry people before. I'd *been*

drunk and angry before. But I was witnessing two distinct meltdowns from Posey and Parker that were epic in their scope and entertaining in their bombast, but were absolutely frightening in their implications for what would happen next. The next hour or so needed to go off with precision and restraint, neither of which was at all possible with those two powder kegs in the room. If the four of us were going to survive, then those two needed to go away. Quickly.

"He was very sweet," Lindsey continued, "and he took on a lot of my grief and my shit, but..."

"He had to drink to numb himself from it?"

"We're complicated people, Dominick, and we keep trying to tell you that."

"And you keep trying to drag me—"

"Nobody's dragging you anywhere, honey," Posey said. "You're a narcissist of the worst variety, the kind who has delusions of humility. It's why I love you, why I will always love you, but why this won't work anymore."

Jesus Christ. What in the hell was I supposed to do with that? She came over to me and grabbed the back of my head and gave me a deep, long kiss then pushed me backward. Pushing Lindsey out of the way as well, she reached into one of the drawers and pulled out a massive black handgun and checked its load, fiddled with it some more, and then pointed it at me.

And at that moment I genuinely thought I was going to die. It seemed like a fitting end to my life story. Desperate to be involved with strong women, but dismal at choosing which ones to involve myself with, I would be killed in the office where my professional wife worked a higher profile and more lucrative job than mine while she was pregnant with another man's child that she wanted to raise without me. Perfect indeed. All I needed to do was throw up and complete the humiliation. But I didn't. And she didn't pull the trigger.

"Come on," I said, with absolutely no conviction behind it. "Put the gun down."

She waved the gun away from me and waved it in the direction of Lindsey and Parker, then back to me.

"All of you. Out."

Parker rolled out of his chair and headed for the door. Lindsey made no such move.

"Put the gun down, you crazy bat. We need everyone—"

"There is no we. Just me right now. I'm going to save you all and move forward and take care of this."

"You sound just like your brother," Lindsey said. "I still miss him."

I looked at Lindsey, then at Parker, then back to Lindsey, trying to get a read on what was happening. But it was Posey who spoke to me.

"Had no idea what you were getting into, did you?"

"Don't do this. You're not your brother. He had…you're different."

"I don't want to be different. I need to be—"

"Remember that time he had that bee hive in his basement?"

Posey smiled and nodded and let the gun dip slightly.

"I don't need to be around for this," Parker said. "I'll be across the street drinking with the baseball rubes."

He didn't close the door when he left but no one made a move to do anything about it.

"He thought he needed to be the one to take care of the

problem himself," Lindsey continued. "He wouldn't call an exterminator, wouldn't let the neighbor help, just wanted to burn the thing down himself."

"I'm allergic to bees and he wanted me to be able to visit."

I had no idea Posey was allergic to bees. How did that never come up? I felt like I was on an episode of *Dr. Phil* that had been hijacked by *America's Most Wanted.*

"And he burned down the fucking house trying to help you. Lesson being, you guys aren't the best at rational problem solving."

"Says the woman whose reaction to a rape was to promise Jesus she'd never sleep with anyone else until she was married and then drunk fucked my brother and decided she had to marry him."

"Says the woman who married a fucking writer who can't do even the most simple task without involving criminals and screwing it up so badly I need to step in and fix it."

They both looked at me. I was smart enough, or confused enough, not to say anything.

"Sometimes you need to burn the house down," Posey said. "Kills the bees and pays out insurance."

"I miss him a lot. Every day."

"But you're going to have a baby with Doofus Number Two?"

"Titus isn't coming back. Maybe I need to burn my house down."

Posey nodded. I had no idea what they were talking about and couldn't figure out if they were speaking metaphorically or if I was in the middle of their planning session for an arson spree. There were no clocks around, everything was on computer monitors and cell phones, so I had no idea how much time had passed and how much closer we were to the twenty-minute deadline, but it had to be getting close.

"I don't want to leave," I said. "I want to see this through. I want to know it's done and I'm safe."

Posey finally dropped the gun to her side in a relaxed, yet frustrated gesture.

"You'll never be safe, Dominick. If it's not this it'll be the next thing. You're your own worst enemy and you're the worst enemy of everyone around you."

"That's not fair."

"Not fair? I'm a bail agent, my brother was a bail agent, a crazy jealous and violent bail agent, my dad was a con man, my uncles are bad guys and bad cops and other losers who carry guns. But they shielded me from the worst of it. They loved me and protected me. Barely a year of knowing you and my brother was murdered, my best friend went full-on serial killer, *I've* been shot at and burned and locked in the trunk of my car, and I almost strangled my godfather to death. That's what's not fair, buddy."

"Morton Taylor is your godfather?"

She pointed to Lindsey.

"Like she already said, we're all complicated people. Except you. You're a disease."

I don't break easily. I bend. I wobble. I collapse and wait for evil to pass over me. But I don't break. Not until my wife calls me a disease. I was so close to getting out of the office before I fell apart, but two men in suits appeared in the doorway and blocked my escape.

Posey must have seen them as well because she put her gun

away.

"About time," she said. "Though I was hoping these two would be gone by now."

I continued staring at the men in suits trying to hold myself together. They were both taller than I was and had similar features. But the one to my left wore a cheap blue suit I recognized from the rack at the local Walmart while the one to my right wore a classier, and I assumed more expensive, charcoal gray suit. He reached into the pocket of that classy suit and pulled out a slim black wallet with a silver badge and a Michigan Department of Corrections ID card.

"Deputy Assistant Director Michael—"

"Don't bother with the badge on him, Uncle Mike, that's my husband and he was just leaving."

Uncle?

"No way," I said. "This concerns me. You have an uncle at the department of corrections and never thought to mention that as we're all being chased around by thugs in DOC uniforms?"

"He's a family friend helping me handle a family matter."

Looking at the two suits and hearing the words come out of her mouth made me feel less awful about her calling me a disease because she was obviously more messed up than I was. Sure I made bad choices and had a lot to learn about staying out of trouble, but she was part of a family that was corrupt to kind of an amazing degree within the freaking state government. I wondered how far it went up. Was it just corrections? Was the governor her stepbrother or maybe she had a cousin or two in Congress?

"This is Detective Chris Holm with the state police," Mike

said, nodding to the guy in the cheap suit. "He helps me with our internal affairs investigations."

"So they're not fake uniforms or stolen uniforms, these are actual corrections officers?"

Mike looked to Posey, I assumed for guidance on how much to reveal to me.

"You really need to get out of here, Dominick. We're going to take care of this. We'll shut this down and you'll survive. Just like you always do."

I shifted back and forth on my feet, wanting to head for the door and be done with it, but also horribly curious about what was going on and what was going to happen. The thought of being on the outside while something exciting went down was more than I could take. I also still held pathetically to the idea that there was still a chance for me to do something big, something important enough to get her back and restore my reputation in her eyes. That certainly wasn't going to happen with me being anywhere else.

Lindsey had no similar concerns or curiosities.

"I need to go grab my future baby's daddy before he drinks himself impotent. You kids have fun storming the castle."

With Lindsey gone, the hostility in the room toward me was overbearing so I finally left as well. I would retreat to my own base camp and rethink my plan and find a way to attack this thing a different way. In my car, trying to figure out exactly where my base camp would be, I saw something that certainly provided a new way to attack the problem, but also scared me shitless. I saw Jay, the quiet brother, go into the building by himself. There were only two reasons for that in my mind:

his brother Charlie, the mouthy loose cannon who had killed the Carter brothers and always seemed ready to explode, was waiting somewhere else to spring a trap; or Jay had gone rogue and was planning something even worse.

I called Lindsey and told her what I saw.

"We're still in the bar drinking," she said. "Come join us."

"I thought you were going to go make a baby."

"That's gross. Don't talk about it. That's between us. Come have a drink."

"We don't have time for that. We need to find that other guard."

"H ave a drink and we'll make a chart if you want."

Something was off in her voice but I couldn't quite figure out what it was. But it was certainly odd that 1) she was still at the bar drinking when she had gone there to get Parker away from there before he killed his sperm with booze and 2) that she was so insistent I join them.

"What's going on, Lindsey? Something's up with you and I can't take being around anyone else messed up right now."

"Parker left me. Said he thought the baby was a bad idea now and doesn't want to see me anymore."

"Ah, crap," I said. "I'm sorry. I'll be right there."

When I went into the bar I couldn't find her. I wandered around for a few minutes before hitting up the bartender to ask if he'd seen her. He nodded and handed me a note scrawled on a bar napkin.

"She gave me a twenty and told me to give this to you if you asked about her."

The note just said: *Get on the bus and take it to The Corner.*

The bartender was gone so I couldn't get any clarification, but really the note was easy enough to follow. The Corner was a longtime nickname for the corner of Michigan and Trumbull Avenues where Tiger Stadium had been until it was closed and then eventually torn down. The bus was the party bus that the bar sponsored that would drive bar patrons across the downtown area to parking spots, hotels, casinos, and even other bars as a sign of goodwill. One of their most popular spots was The Corner, where tourists and locals alike would run the base paths and play catch on the field that was still preserved by a weird cult-like society that held out hope for some kind of baseball museum on the spot instead of the mixed use commercial development everyone assumed would be built.

What I couldn't figure out was why Lindsey was leading me on some kind of wild goose chase out there. I had a vague idea and didn't like what it implied at all. Back during my previous adventure, I'd had an enlightening, if surreal, conversation with Rickard at The Corner right before we drove out to a storage shed with the body of a security guard he had killed earlier that morning in the trunk. That recollection mixed with all of the other bombshells that had dropped recently, it made sense there was some kind of a connection. And the only way I would know would be to get on the bus.

The baseball game had already begun so the crowd on the bus had thinned considerably and I was able to get a seat by myself in the back of the bus. I rested my head on the window and watched the battered scenery of the edge of downtown pass by as the bus made stop after stop before finally pulling in front of the field. I got off the bus slowly and wondered if I would be assaulted right away or if it would happen after the bus pulled away. Instead, I saw Lindsey and Parker standing with a grossly obese man I vaguely recognized, waving at me.

"The team is assembled once more," the fat man said. "Such cloak-and-dagger assembly to wit. Do you feel the energy?"

I looked at Lindsey.

"You told me he left you."

She shrugged her shoulders and smirked.

"You didn't want to meet me. I had to try something else. So I played to your sensitive hero complex."

"You don't remember me, do you?" the fat man said.

"We talked about this, Dominick," Parker said. "Earlier. Your great marketing plan?"

It was coming into focus. He'd been fat the last time I saw him but he was even more so now.

"Ellis Meany," I said. "About my book. Er, our book."

"Books, yes," he said, slapping hands together. "*Many* books together. It will be fabulous."

Lindsey smiled awkwardly and took Parker's hand. The three of them strolled away from me toward the field and I followed. When we reached the spot where home plate had been, the four of us gathered around the diamond-shaped dirt cutout.

"What's going on? Why are we talking about books when we should be looking for that crazy guard?"

"If we're going to really do this thing right," Parker said, "Lindsey and I, my current situation isn't going to cut it."

"Professors can't raise kids?"

"When Ellis generously funded our fellowship program, it was just for the one year with the possibility of further funding if he and the trustees agreed there were mutual benefits for its continuation."

"Okay…"

"Our friend is being political here," Ellis said. "I wanted to see if the pair of you would rise to your promise or flame out and take my reputation and my money with you."

"Oh," I said.

"Yes, oh," Parker said. "Your performance has certainly been a disappointment and I haven't exactly been setting the literary world on fire either."

"No, no no," Ellis said. "I don't like this negativity. Yes, there were *things*. Things in the past. Things even now. But we have an opportunity here, the three of us, for something… immense."

"Why are we out here then instead of back at the school?"

"So many questions and so little time for them. Let's focus on the promise here and where we go next."

"With our book?"

Parker jerked his thumb at me.

"You're sure you want him involved? His verbal skills still leave—"

Ellis ran at me and grabbed me with one arm and pulled Parker toward us with his other beefy arm and wrapped us up to his chest.

"We three...only together can we—"

I pushed away from the hug and stomped my foot in the dirt.

"Enough of the babble and the platitudes and the rainbow smoke up our asses. Get to the point so we can get on in the real world."

Ellis dropped his arm from Parker and his jowls melted into a sad plateau. Parker and Lindsey stepped back from him, further away from me.

"*This* is your world," Lindsey said. "You have no business in the real world. Your wife, your...whatever she is now, she has it covered. Her family has it—"

"I'm the only witness to that asshole blowing away two people. I'm not part of her family now, if I ever was, and that leaves me, that leaves all of us, vulnerable."

Lindsey was swaying back and forth, still holding Parker's hand, and on one of her sways away from me, I noticed she had a small backpack slung over her shoulder. I hadn't seen her with it when she was at the office and my stomach dropped when I realized what she likely had in there. I only had her word that she had redirected the shipment before I showed up. In fact, we only had her word that the box hadn't arrived that morning like I expected. She could have easily signed for it and had Parker fake my signature. I'm sure the UPS guy wouldn't have asked for ID. He wasn't delivering packages for the CIA or the NSA.

But why? And why pull me over here to talk about books while she had the nuclear MacGuffin on her back? Was it a trap? Why not stop driving myself insane and just ask?

"What's in the backpack?"

"Don't worry about it. Talk with the boys about your books. It all sounds very exciting."

I reached out to grab the backpack and Parker made a move to step in front of her to block me, but Lindsey was quick enough on her own and spun around and avoided my grab.

"You're going to get them all killed," I said. "When he shows up and they don't have—"

"They have guns, Dominick. Three grown ass adults with guns and training against one unsuspecting moron."

"He's not a moron. These guys are psychopaths."

"My god, you're so thick. They were going to kill those two guys all along. From the moment they became involved, that was the only outcome. You can't say you didn't try. It was a valiant effort and you can rest easy knowing you weren't complicit in it but it's done."

I turned to run away and realized that's why she had dragged me out here. So I couldn't go back. It was at least a thirty-minute walk back to the office from where we were and because the baseball game had already started, the party bus would only be coming by once an hour. I was stuck. I ran anyway.

Between my poor shape and lack of substantial knowledge of the downtown area away from campus, it took me almost an hour to get back to the office. I had no idea what I expected to find or what I hoped to do as I ran up the stairs, but I was still shocked to see Posey sitting at her desk moving paperwork around like everything was just peachy. When she saw me, though, she broke down crying. Three steps into the office, I saw why. The bodies of Uncle Mike and Chris Holm were sprawled across the floor in pools of blood.

"He was so quick," she said. "I knew he was ruthless but I thought with three of us we'd be okay."

"Did you call the police? This can't just be about the sample."

She shook her head.

"He killed his brother. He's killing everyone."

"Everyone except you."

"Because he can't."

"The will?"

She nodded.

"Even if he's in prison for murder?"

"He'll be a king in prison. Family connections. Money. Power."

"And what about you?"

"I'll run the business from out here. It's what they always wanted."

"Does he know Lindsey and Parker have the sample?"

"He didn't ask. He didn't care. I'm sure he'll find them too."

"And me?"

"I tried to save you from this."

"What am I supposed to do now? Run away?"

"He won't chase you. You're not the father. You can go to New York. Live your dream."

"While you take over this criminal empire?"

She continued shuffling the paper around then threw all of it into a trash can.

"It's better than being unemployed or working a crappy job."

"I need to tell Lindsey and Parker."

"You can't save them, Dominick. Save yourself."

I bounced on the balls of my feet and tried to will my brain to come up with a plan or anything that would make the situation better but all I got was a line.

"I'm not the disease, you're the disease."

I called Lindsey's cell phone but she didn't answer. That wasn't surprising. My guess is she knew more about what was happening than I did and was holding out hoping that she'd come up with something to save herself and Parker. They would be fine. I needed to save myself. And maybe in saving myself I could save everyone else.

My god, Posey was right about that too. I *am* a narcissist.

I might as well use that, right?

By the time I got back down to the street again my luck with my illegal parking job had run out and my Zipcar had been towed away. The fines associated with that would be murder for me and probably bar me from ever using a Zipcar again, but one of my strengths is pushing unfortunate information like that down to the depths of my brain and ignoring the worst parts of my life. It also helped me push down nagging thoughts of the lack of police involvement and what that meant for me. I'd seen enough of Posey's evil tricks to fully believe she could make two dead bodies go away with no trouble, but I also wondered if she also had the pull, and malice, to pin those bodies on me. There were pieces of me all over that office and it wouldn't be hard to make it look like I went crazy.

This was one of those times I wished I had more police contacts I could trust. But if I believed Posey and her family had the pull to clean up the bodies and/or frame me for it, I had to also wonder how much help I would get from a random detective I had no connection with if I popped into police headquarters and told them my story. This was where I had to ride my narcissism for all it was worth and think very hard about what made me special and what strengths I had to use to fix this.

That's all I thought about as I made my way across the street and up the stairs of the parking garage to where Posey and I kept our cars and by the time I got into my own car for the first time in what seemed like forever, the only thing I could point to as my strength was as a writer but couldn't figure out any way to use that to bring down a criminal enterprise. If I had stuck with my brief pursuit of journalism it would maybe be a different story. I'd seen a number of Detroit criminal institutions brought down by journalists even in this day of declining revenue and declining readership. But I'd never had the killer instinct for journalism. I'd never had the taste for blood they needed to bring down institutions. All I ever wanted to do was use my access and my writing to make friends and get perks and seem important.

Holy shit.

That's it.

I ran back across the street and almost all the way to the

office to tell Posey my plan before I thought better of it and, for once, showed some restraint. If my crazy idea was really going to work I needed to do some planning. I needed to have the perfect pitch rather than my normal half-baked ideas. So I left through the back exit and returned to my car then parked across the street from the office and waited for Posey to come out so I could follow her. I tried to picture myself as a slick PI on a stakeout to save the heroine but I couldn't shake the feeling that I was nothing more than a Peeping Tom spying on his wife.

It was passing the three-hour mark when I finally saw her emerge from the main entrance. One of the reasons I had chosen the parking spot I did was because it had a good view of all three exits from the building. I expected her to come out either the back entrance or the side entrance because they provided easier access to the parking garage and avoided the worst of the tourist congestion on Woodward. The only good reason to come out of the front exit was…

Crap.

She crossed the street against traffic and was making a straight line for my parking spot. There was no reason I should have been scared of my wife, but I was terrified and was paralyzed between starting my car and trying to drive away or staying where I was and facing her down and telling her my entire plan (or what of it I'd managed to develop in my head while I was waiting for her) and hoping she'd jump on board. Instead, she weaved through the cars creating a path away from me but that was more direct to the ticket window behind me at Comerica Park.

When she had passed by me I got out of my car and watched her to see if she was indeed going to the baseball park and got my answer when she went to the Will Call window. I'd never known my wife to be a sports fan of any kind, let alone something as cerebral and boring as baseball, but at this point I was convinced everything I knew about her was a lie so I wasn't going to be surprised by anything. The fact that this family and their creepiness seemed so linked to baseball was starting to have an effect on my burgeoning interest in the game as well so my emotions were decidedly mixed, to say the least, as I followed Posey into the stadium. The game had just concluded, another extra innings gem wasted by the bullpen according to the drunken cheap seat prognosticators on their way out of the stadium, so getting inside was a breeze.

I made it into the stadium just in time to see Posey head to my left past the food court and the first batch of concession stands toward the main set of stairs to the upper levels. She kept walking past the stairs all the way to the end of the concourse where she went into the elevator area set aside for suite holders. As much as I want to believe otherwise, I am not quick on my feet so I didn't think I had a chance of talking my way onto the elevator and that was okay.

I'd been up to one of the suites once for a work event and while they were very nice on the surface—lots of marble and plush carpeting and shiny silver serving trays of hot dogs, sausages, and chips—it was a smaller space with fewer people and much, much harder to stay in the background and spy on everyone. I was already in the stadium and it was a beautiful day with great smells around me and the cheers of the crowd to buoy my spirits. If I was going to spy on my wife, this seemed like a much better place to do it than from a stuffy car.

So I found a picnic table far enough away to protect me but

close enough to still see the comings and goings of the elevator people and waited. And waited. Then some more waiting. This led my overanalytical mind to start drawing conclusions between then and the last time I had been in the baseball stadium right before Lindsey found me and dragged me into this mess. I may not have handled everything that came next the best way possible, but that was the trigger moment and I had lost track of that as things spun further and further out of control. From the very beginning I was a pawn between the competing desires of Lindsey and Posey. Lindsey took an active role in guilting me into action and Posey took a more hands-off approach and waited in the background for me to do what I do best and mess things up.

It was one more I time I realized I wasn't the narrator or hero of my own story. I wasn't even Watson telling the story of Sherlock Holmes as a respected equal. I was found footage providing color commentary and an alternate angle at most in an epic story that I was only peripherally involved with. It was the same story with the girls at work I had been asking about at the ball game who were spying on me. I was just a pawn between them and our boss for control of the administrative fiefdom in the department.

Thinking of pawns triggered some repressed memories from my brief involvement with the school chess team. I'd always been a smart kid, and even as I got older and my laziness and poor decision making had more of an effect on my grades than my intelligence, everyone around me assumed I was smarter than I really was. This led to invitations to things like Math Club and Science Club and things I had no interest in and which would provide immediate proof of my inferior intelligence. But

I succumbed for one year to Chess Club because they had a trip to New York City planned. I remembered a few things about pawn strategy because I always saw promoting the pawn as an easy way to avoid learning any other strategy.

In my current situation I was an isolated pawn. I was on my way across the board to be promoted to a queen but I had no support from the pieces around me. In this situation the best way to turn it from a weakness into a strength is to keep the pawn moving and put pressure on the side in endgame hoping that they make a fatal mistake. I knew both sides were in endgame so I needed to stay moving and put pressure on them and wait for the mistakes I could capitalize on.

The sudden thunder of crowd noise and people swarming around me was my first clue that the game was over and no one had come out of the elevator room. I had to get up from my table and move with the crowd closer to the elevator room to keep an eye on who was coming out, and it was in the middle of the second wave of exiting baseball fans that I saw Posey leave. She was quickly followed by Lindsey and Parker, who were holding hands and smiling in a way that hinted they weren't in nearly as much danger as I thought they were. I was fine with that though. I'd long suspected they were colluding against me; this was just more proof.

I'd put enough pressure on them; now it was time to put pressure on the other side and see what happened. I had an idea that if it worked right it would get me promoted to queen and provide me safety for the rest of the game. I made my way quickly back to my car and headed toward the suburbs again, this time making a stop at the first big chain bookstore I came across. There was a tattooed and spiked woman with a giant name tag that said PENELOPE on it standing behind the information desk when I approached. She smiled while I stood there unable to wrap my mind around what I was looking for.

"Uh, I'm looking for stuff about poison," I said, looking, I'm sure, shady as hell. "Undetectable, like iocane powder."

She locked her eyes on mine and as uncomfortable as it made me, I knew it would be worse if I looked away.

"Like from *The Princess Bride*?"

"Sort of. Not fictional poisons but poisons used in fiction. For murder."

"I'm not sure by law I should be—"

"I'm a writer," I said. "It's for research."

Like that should explain everything.

"Mmmmm-hmmm," she said.

I watched to see if she would go for the phone and call the police, but she walked around from behind the desk and waved for me to follow her.

"So you're looking for cozies?"

"I have no idea what that means," I said, running every word through my head before it left my mouth to make sure I wouldn't incriminate myself any further.

Once again realizing that, for a writer, I was woefully under-read, even in the genre I professed my allegiance to. In fact, my presence in a bookstore was rather rare unto itself. I never had money for books so I checked most of my reading out of the library or bought in paperback from thrift stores.

"Like Agatha Christie," she said. "Though these days it's less about the method of death and more about the hobby of the detective."

I had no idea what any of those words meant in this context, but I didn't care. She led me to the back corner of the store and waved her hands in the general direction of two shelves.

"We don't have a separate section just for cozies, but if you look at the mass markets that's where you'll find most of them. A lot of it is repetitive, but some of them are really good. You just gotta put in the time to find the diamonds."

"Sure. Right. Of course," I said. "Thanks so much."

"And if you really want a jolt, the true crime section is back over there."

She stared at me again uncomfortably for another second and then walked away. As I strolled back and forth along the shelves, running my index finger over the pastel paperbacks with punny titles and an abundance of food and pets on the covers, I started to see the wave of flaws in my initial plan. There was no way I could read through enough of these books quickly enough to develop the base of knowledge I would need for covert domestic assassination. The true crime section provided more of what I needed for the initial part of my plan. And that was really the most important part anyway.

I grabbed five different books I thought I would need to make my case and paid for them with a gift card I got for taking a survey at the hospital that I had been afraid to cash until then for fear it was counterfeit. But the clerk smiled, asked me if I wanted a receipt, and sent me on my way. I backtracked a few miles to the big house on the lake where Posey had almost strangled Morton Taylor to death and knocked on the door then rang the doorbell. I don't think Jay Taylor immediately recognized me until he pulled a gun and put it to my head. I slowly pulled two of the books out of the shopping bag and held them out to him.

"I don't want to die," I said. "And I really don't want to kill you either. But I think I can make you famous."

Jay Taylor didn't say anything, he just grabbed my arm and pulled me along behind him as he fled the house. He dragged me out into the street toward a beat up old Volvo station wagon. I was relieved there was no trunk to put me in as Taylor got into the driver's seat and motioned for me to get in on the other side. There was no coercion, he didn't have a gun on me, but I got in anyway. I'd failed in scheme after scheme to split him off from his brother and talk to him, this seemed like the best chance I was ever going to get for that before things went completely to hell.

I was tense though for the first few blocks, wondering if he was just driving me away from the house in a burner car so he could shoot me and dump me in a weedy lot, but once we emerged from the neighborhoods onto a main highway I relaxed a bit. If he was going to kill me it was going to be as part of a longer plan and, ever the optimist, I saw that as a good thing as it gave me time to either talk him out of it or, if I had to, take him out myself.

"Posey and I talked about this before," he said. "She even took a crack at it once but said she was too close to it. Whatever that means."

I nodded, trying desperately to keep my mouth shut long enough for the silences to do their work and keep him talking.

"But with Mort on his way out and the stuff with Little Mort, well, we've got an interesting story to tell. Kind of Shakespearean if you think about it."

I nodded again. So much I wanted to say though. I wanted to bring up the show *Justified* and talk about how the villainous families were almost as popular as the lead character Raylan Givens. But I didn't. Just nodded like a bobblehead. Unfortunately, I drew the quiet brother instead of the chatty one and he was pretty good at keeping his mouth shut. At one point that would have made me feel better because the chatty brother was the violent one, but after the carnage I saw left in Posey's office after Jay showed up I realized quiet didn't mean safe.

"So where are we going?" I asked.

"I've got this place out in the Irish Hills that nobody knows about. No time to get started like right now. Right?"

*It's a trap.*

That's all I could think. That's all that made sense. Though none of this made sense. Why drive me all the way out to some old touristy trap area just to kill me? Was he going to torture me? I'd have thought he'd had enough exposure to me to know I was no font of juicy secrets or useful information. If he wanted to kill Posey he could have done it when he killed everyone else in her office. He didn't need to set a trap for her and use me as bait. So maybe this was one of those cases where the simplest answer was the right answer.

"This is like a retreat then," I said. "A writing retreat?"

"Yes," he said with too much enthusiasm. "You, me, your books, and my stories. We've got a bunch of booze up there and some canned food or some ramen noodles or some shit like that to eat. We can stop for anything we don't have. Do you need pens or paper or anything? I think there's a typewriter maybe."

"Uh, I usually work on my laptop but when I'm stuck I like those cheap stick pens and spiral notebooks."

"Sure. Sure," he said. "We'll see what they have at the general store when we get there. They got a bunch of stuff but it kind of shifts, you know, based on what they get out there. This is tourist season, which is hard, probably not the ideal time to be out there, but it's quieter than here and, like I said, nobody knows about it."

Yes. He'd said that a number of times and I wondered what he meant by it.

"Back at the office, I saw you going up to see Posey and her uncle on my way out."

"Shit," he said.

I waited to see if he was going to say anything else but he didn't.

"Posey said you spared her because of your dad's will," I said. "Are you going to take it out on me?"

He smiled. It creeped me out and he did it again.

"Posey said I *spared* her?"

"Because of the will."

"When things settle down you and your wife need to have a long talk."

"I don't think she wants to be my wife anymore."

He nodded his head and twisted his lip up contemplatively.

"No, I'd guess she probably wouldn't. Gotta say she made an effort for you though. You must be somebody special to her."

I wanted to keep him talking but I was certain I didn't want to know anything else he could tell me about Posey. This was a golden opportunity if I played it smart and kept my mouth shut and my ears open.

Ha.

I figured things would be quiet for the rest of the ride considering I hadn't heard a single word from this guy in the several times I'd met him, but I guessed he must not have been silent by choice around his brother because he talked the *entire* length of the drive. He rambled on about traffic, the design of the American highway system, and how much he loved sugar, among other topics. There was an interesting side tangent from the highway system speech about the failures of the American auto industry and its links to his own family troubles that I hoped would turn into something good, but the best that came of it was finding out he had placed a UAW sticker on the bumper of his Volvo when he bought it to make a point.

I felt a brief moment of sympathy for anyone who had ever endured one of my own long rants, though I hoped…*hoped,* I was more focused and less ranty when I talked. Finally, though, after about an hour and a half, he stopped long enough for me to say something.

"Is that the general store you were talking about?"

We'd exited the highway a few minutes ago and been dumped into the dilapidated tourist area known as the Irish Hills. Once a resort area popular with travelers between Detroit and Chicago, it, like everything else that had once been nice in this state, had been shit on by the economy and changing vacation tastes. It still had a robust tourist trade but it had moved out to the area by the NASCAR track and into the hidden areas along the lakes where millionaires replaced family cottages with massive glassed in eyesores. But even asshole millionaires needed gas for their SUVs and personal water crafts and even the most well-prepared stock car tailgater needed a last-minute snack or DVD rental for the RV, so the building Jay had turned into at such a sharp turn that I thought my seat belt would crush my kidneys, was the only one along this strip of US-12 that still seemed occupied.

"Yes. Good call. I was going to wait until after we passed by the prehistoric forest but…well, I don't want to spoil anything so let's just get what you need and maybe go to the bathroom because I'm not sure how the plumbing has been since the last time I was back here."

Maybe I wouldn't need to worry about finding ways to kill him, if needed, with poisoned cookies or milk that tastes like bitter almonds or whatever. We'd both die from methane poisoning from backed up toilets. Jay went to the bathroom first and I initially went to wander around and look for anything I could use for writing, but I found myself instead moving out to the parking lot and standing roughly halfway between his car and the door wondering if I should steal it and drive away. Drive to Chicago. Drive to Wisconsin. Drive to Florida or Texas or Los Angeles.

And wait to die there?

I was in endgame; the pieces were moving in a way I could visualize; this was the best chance I was ever going to get to try for an outcome that wouldn't completely suck.

Just keep my mouth shut. Keep my ears open. And don't do anything stupid.

"Hey, whatcha doing out here?"

Like make him suspicious.

"I get carsick easily," I said, with the full conviction of a nauseated stomach and dizziness. "Just needed to get more of this fresh air."

"While staring at my car like you want to steal it?"

"Staring at it like I'm wondering where in there I could throw up, if it came to that, without ruining anything."

Awkward silence. Waiting to see if he buys it.

Waiting.

"Spoken like a true road warrior," he finally said. "I used to barf all the time when I was a kid and we'd drive up north in the summer and over Christmas."

"I actually haven't been on many road trips. Probably why I never got over this."

"Only way to get over it is drive instead of being a passenger. Unless you're my brother."

When he said that, he looked off into the distance like I'd seen parodied in so many movies. And then he was silent again. It's like his body was choking on the ability to speak for so long without being interrupted and didn't know how to handle it. I noted that and hoped to find a way to use it to my advantage in the future.

"I need to go in and get pencils," I said. "And a notebook. Notepad, actually. I prefer not to have—"

"They have a laptop in there if you want that instead. It's a little thing, probably more for watching movies and checking email for people who don't know how to take a vacation, but let's go in and have a look."

I didn't care anything about watching movies, but email might be handy to have so I followed him back into the store to a counter in the back that sold several different kinds of portable technology. Folks like Jay mentioned, who didn't know how to take a vacation, could choose from a variety of music players, three different models of portable DVD players, several CB radio systems, and one single option at a laptop. It was a black brick roughly the size of a hardcover book and seemed very flimsy and cheap when I held it in my hands. There was no way I wanted to do any typing on it but I was still thinking about the other things I could use it for.

"I don't see an Ethernet connection anywhere," I said. "Does it have Wi-Fi capability?"

The clerk looked at me with a mix of contempt and confusion but Jay piped in and shut the whole thing down.

"No internet," he said, shoving the computer back into the clerk's hands. "This was a mistake. Let's go. I'm sure we can find a pen or something to write with at the cabin."

He stomped out of the store and I followed behind him at a safe distance, not exactly sure what had happened to make him so mad. Was he worried I would be distracted? Was this thing really that important to him? Or was he worried about me having access to the outside world through email and ruining his secret plan? It still seemed like a lot of effort to bring me all the way out here just to kill me when he hadn't had any problem gunning down two more dangerous dudes than me right in front of Posey. Not that it mattered anyway in the bigger scheme of things. Just stick to the plan: mouth shut, ears open.

"I've been burned too many times by losing work on my computer," I said when I got in the car. "So I started saving my stuff to cloud drives like—"

"No, it's fine. I just want to make sure...this environment out here is very important to me. The isolation is part of that and technology is the enemy of that."

"Sure. I have no problem writing like that, with the retreat vibe you were talking about. It was just that *you* were the one who mentioned the laptop so—"

"We're good. Fine."

And with that he pulled off the road with another ridiculously sharp turn and barreled over ruts and dodged trees until he slammed the brakes right before hitting a giant red dinosaur head.

"Holy shit," I yelled, before being snapped back into submission by my seat belt.

"Go look at it," Jay said. "There's more of them out there."

"More dinosaur heads?"

"It's not just the heads," he said, getting out of the car and heading around to the back. "It's the whole body. There's five or six of them out there."

I took a few tentative steps toward the head in front of me and noticed there was indeed an entire giant red body attached to it. At one point it looked like the dinosaur had been standing upright, king of this weird tourist forest, but now he was tipped over, fading and failing with his face in the dirt, something I could certainly relate to.

"What is this place?"

"The Irish Hills Prehistoric Forest," he said from behind me. "It used to be an amusement park with a volcano and a waterslide back in the day. The very first girl I ever had sex with is part of the family that owns it. She owns the cabin we're going to as well."

I turned back to see if he was telling me the truth and came face-to-face with the barrel of a shotgun.

"Tell me what the fuck you're really doing out here with me," Jay said.

"You brought me out here."

"All of this time we were chasing you and you were a little bitch, why did you suddenly change your mind and want to be my partner?"

"I don't know. I'm out of options. I'm freaking out," I said. "Can you put the gun down?"

He pushed the gun further into my forehead until I squatted down on the ground in front of him. I felt the pressure ease after a second and thought he was going to pull the gun away, but he was reaching into his pocket for something that he threw at me. It was one of the pastel cozy books I bought at the bookstore. I had unfortunately left the cozy books, my research for methods for ways to kill Jay Taylor, in the same bag as the true crime books I planned to use to make my case to Jay Taylor that he should trust me to be close to him while writing his life story.

The book that bounced off my arm and landed in the dirt next to the dinosaur head was an affront to all of that trust.

"Tell me why you're really here."

"I want to write," I said. "I was telling the truth. I need money. I want to make money doing this, a lot of money, and those books are the way to do it in this field these days. But you have to write to a very specific formula and the best way to learn that formula is to read a bunch of these books at once."

I waited for him to shoot me. When he didn't, I continued.

"Things are so fucked up with Posey. I don't know who she is anymore or what she's up to and I'm sick of just waiting around for somebody to come and kill me. I bought all of these books with the best of intentions to either write one of these series about a guy like me involved with a gangster for a wife or to become the ghostwriter for whoever answered the door at that house. Maybe, ideally, both."

I waited again for the bang. Again, no bang.

"You aren't going to try and kill me?" he asked.

"I honestly had no idea you would even be at that house. After what you did at Posey's office I figured you'd be long gone."

"What *I* did at Posey's office?"

Things started clicking and I didn't like the picture that was developing.

"Posey killed them, didn't she? And you were running away from her when I caught up to you? That's why we're out here. Off the grid."

Jay dropped the gun to his side and I stood up but wasn't ready to try and move toward him yet.

"I'm hungry, you want to get some food?"

I nodded yes and the ordeal was over. The shotgun went into the back of the Volvo and Jay and I went into the front and we backed out of the abandoned prehistoric forest onto the dirt road and drove in silence until we pulled onto a never-ending driveway that stopped at a trailer home that had seen better days. When he asked if I wanted food I assumed we'd stop somewhere considering he said there was nothing but ramen, canned food, and booze inside, but I sure as hell wasn't going to push the point after the debacle in the woods. Jay left the shotgun in the car, but as we walked up the lumpy gravel path to the big porch I couldn't stop thinking about it and how dangerous it could be for me even if it wasn't inside with us.

Thinking about sleeping in the same trailer as Jay, with or without a shotgun nearby, also made me realize I had no extra clothes or any other supplies for an extended stay. It really wasn't a big deal and there had been an entire year of grad school where I couch surfed at friends' apartments and never bothered with a change of clothes, but that extended an intimacy and familiarity to this situation and to Jay Taylor that I was not at all comfortable with.

Inside the trailer was musty and stale and I choked back a gag or two upon entering. There was a small kitchen and dining area to the right that was decorated straight out of the '60s and the further into the trailer you moved, the further in time you moved as well. The living room to the left of where we were standing was full-scale 1970s décor, and we're not talking vintage or kitschy but actual, still remaining from the 1970s décor down to the green shag carpet and an orange corduroy couch with a giant crocheted blanket draped over the back, leading to a hallway paneled in that special 1980s basement style I remembered so well.

"You mentioned food," I said. "You also mentioned there was only ramen and canned goods here."

"And booze. I believe I said booze too."

"It doesn't seem like anyone has been in here in…a while. Are you sure it's still good?"

"We'll get a pizza, don't worry about it. But there's a giant thing of Spaghetti-Os in the pantry there that I'm sure would taste just as good now as when they were first canned."

"I've always had a weak spot for Spaghetti-Os, especially the ones with meatballs."

Jay Taylor smiled brightly and bounced a few times on his feet.

"Me too. My mom always bought the kind with the hot dogs in them and I thought that was so gross. I always picked them out."

And with that opening salvo, the tension eased, the laughter increased, and the processed pasta products flowed freely. While I opened the giant can with an old-school manual can opener, Jay dug through the lower level cabinets, assembling the liquor bottles he found along the small kitchen table where I was working on the can.

"I don't see a microwave anywhere," I said. "Does the stove work?"

"I honestly don't know. I've never used it."

"Are there spoons anywhere?"

"Spoons, yes. I think there might even be a bowl or two. This place isn't exactly set up for full-on entertaining."

I wanted to ask what it was used for, but I found a spoon in my hand and my hunger overtook, reverting me back to being an elementary school kid on summer vacation trying to get lunch over with as quickly as possible so I could get back outside and play. I dug my spoon directly into the can and scooped a big glob of pasta into my mouth. Jay laughed and followed suit then pushed a black box in my direction.

"This stuff is pretty rough as far as red wine goes," he said. "But it seems like the perfect complement to cold canned pasta."

We dug in and quickly disposed of both the Spaghetti-Os and the wine. Jay seemed to ease up and relished my presence more; I, on the other hand, was more aware and more paranoid than ever. I was woozy from the lack of fresh air, but had the focus to look at everything in the kitchen as a weapon. There were six different liquor bottles lined up across the table from where I was sitting and I was sizing each of them up for weight and heft, wondering which I could hit Jay in the head with and kill him the fastest. In addition to the spoons we were both holding, Jay had uncovered two butter knives and a giant carving knife. These were on the counter next to the small, rusting sink.

Since I first started writing crime fiction I'd always looked at everyday items as potential weapons, but always in an academic sense rather than a practical, homicidal sense. Posey was full of shit. All of the bad stuff that had happened to her since we'd been together was her fault, not mine. She was the disease and I'd caught it. She was a killer and I was about to become one as well.

But it was self-defense, right?

"That's what she wants me to think," I said, accidentally out loud.

"What?"

Jay cocked his head in my direction in a sloppy motion that made him the perfect target at that moment if I could settle on a weapon.

"Posey is full of shit," I said, liking how it sounded outside of my head.

"It took you a box of cheap wine and some sketchy kids pasta to realize that?"

"I'm famous in certain circles for how long it takes me to come to simple conclusions."

"I do remember hearing something along those lines about you."

I wanted to ask him so many questions about his family but I couldn't wrap my mind around anything other than murder as survival. Preemptive strike. My Fox News–loving parents were always cheering on that policy for the military; had I inherited those beliefs or been infected with them secondhand? What other horrible beliefs had I come away from that upbringing with? I'd already seen my racist side pop up a number of times; would science denial come next? Did I have any thoughts on climate change?

But I loved my parents. Mostly. And there was much to admire about conservative fiscal policies if they were implemented properly and you could ever separate them from the wacky social issues. Jesus, my head was starting to spin away from me. Maybe that's what I needed. Double down on the woozy and see if I could drink myself to sleep and be done with these weird thoughts.

Or better yet: I could get Jay to drink with me and eat more crappy canned food until he choked to death and the threat was eliminated without me needing to be the executioner.

"Let's crack into the rest of that booze," I said. "I want to start with that scotch. I think that's scotch. Right?"

"Are you okay?"

"Just thinking of the full impact of trickle-down economics," I said. "Freaked myself out."

"Oooookay."

"I just wonder sometimes how much of my troubles are really my own fault or how much is the result of factors outside of my control, like my upbringing or my crazy wife's behind-the-scenes scheming."

"I haven't had much…interaction with you," Jay said, slowly. "But I know your wife and I think I know a thing or two about you too."

I waited for him to finish his thought but he didn't. He scooted his chair out from the table very loudly and very deliberately and picked up the bottle of Johnny Walker Red on the other end of the table. It was the bottle I'd noted to myself was the one that would work best as a weapon because it was thick and square and I knew from experience that it was easy to grip. He brought the bottle back to where he'd been sitting and put it down in front of me but didn't sit down.

"You don't know anything about me," I said.

"I know you won't drink this with me without glasses, just passing the bottle back and forth."

"That's gross. That's not just me."

"No, you're right. Me too. But I know that most of this is still your fault. The you parts at least."

"The *me* parts?"

"Your part in all of this. Your role. Your pieces."

I grunted then said, "Do we *have* any glasses here?"

He stared at me with something between a frown and a smirk and I stared back, looking for any edge I could find while I waited for inspiration, luck, or fate to do me a favor. When he couldn't get the rise out of me he'd been looking for, Jay spun crisply on his heels in a move that 1) indicated he was likely more sober and clear-headed than he was letting on and 2) belied some previous military experience that made sense but also made me very nervous, and then he took two large steps back to the cabinets he'd found the liquor in and made as much noise down there as possible before coming back up with two tumblers that I didn't realize until he put one in front of me were vintage *Star Wars* glasses from the '80s. I popped upright in my seat and dragged my seat with my butt as close to the table as I could get and pulled the glass to my face.

"Holy shit," I said reverently. "My mom had these when I was a kid and it was the only thing she ever had that I thought was cool. I accidentally broke them all a few years later throwing a tantrum and our family never had anything cool ever again."

"My mom worked at Burger King long enough to get us the *Empire Strikes Back* versions and stayed through long enough to bring us home Alf dolls too. Then she said fuck it and left my dad and our family. I still have the Alf doll somewhere with the guitar."

"Oh. Wow."

"I think there was probably more to her leaving than the job though. That's just what I remember of it."

"Right. Sure. Let's get these suckers loaded with some Johnny and put them to good use."

He filled each glass halfway with scotch and we drank quickly then refilled again. Those drinks were longer sips and garnished with more conversation between drinks. We talked about our schooling, our family lives, and our professional lives. Then we talked about Posey and things took a turn for the dark. Jay grew darker in his conversational tone and more aggressive in his movements. He mentioned suicide twice and I immediately thought of the shotgun in the Volvo. Would I still be a killer if I used my words to talk him into doing something to himself rather than him just doing it himself?

"I need some fresh air again," I said. "I'll be back in a minute."

I stepped onto the porch and took a deep breath my body wasn't ready for. The fresh air rattled my lungs and I coughed violently as I approached the steps down to the driveway. Mixed with my drunken stupor and residual dizziness from the stale air inside, my internal equilibrium didn't stand a chance of keeping me upright. I fell down the steps and rolled off into the grass and waited to die. And then I tried to stand up and *wished* to die. I don't know how long I lay in the grass before I tried to stand again, but it seemed like forever. Long enough for my body to have recovered because it wasn't nearly as hard. I was digging through the back of the Volvo looking for the shotgun when I heard a car pulling up the driveway behind me.

The gun was under a flap in the back meant to cover the spare tire, but the mat was stuck and I couldn't get it lifted up enough to get the gun out. I yanked on it as hard as I could and when it finally broke free the momentum spun me around and I stumbled down the driveway toward the oncoming car with the shotgun pointed out. When the car came into sight it stopped. Neither of us moved for several seconds and the driver flashed the headlights twice. I took a step toward the car with the gun still pointed out and the car sped backward down the driveway and out of sight. I stayed there with the gun still pointed that way until I was sure the car wasn't coming back then went back inside and found Jay passed out on the kitchen floor.

Now was my moment.

I moved slowly and carefully between the counters that made up the de facto entry into the kitchen and kept the shotgun out in front of me, slightly raised so Jay couldn't grab it if he was tricking me and playing dead. I moved with a sidestep to keep my eye on the door as well as on Jay on the floor with the stove and kitchen sink to my back. When I was standing over Jay, I was tempted to poke him with the shotgun, but I was still unsure if he was playing a prank on me, lying in wait for me, or if he was legitimately down. I could see faint movement in his chest so I knew he was still alive.

The question was whether I had the nerve to do anything about it.

He groaned a few more times and then tried to stand up with little success. On his third try, when he was about to fall back down again, I held my arm out and pulled him to his feet.

"Must have fallen out of the chair," he said, rubbing his ass with one hand and his face with the other.

"After all that talk, before I went outside," I said, trying not to make it obvious I was holding the shotgun. "Just made me wonder if you had done something about it."

"About what?"

"The stuff you were talking about. Your feelings. Your

depression."

"Why do you have my shotgun?"

"I heard something outside. Thought it was someone coming up the driveway."

"And you were going to shoot it?"

"It was a car," I said, for some reason feeling the need to defend myself from his accusatory tone even though he was lying on the floor drunk. "I stood at the top of the driveway and pointed the gun at them and they drove away."

"Jesus," he said. "You're going to get us killed. Or arrested."

I put the shotgun on the table and sat down on the floor next to him.

"Last year around Christmas I came as close as going to the store and getting some rope and something to stand on that would be sturdy," I said. "My worst fear is always that I'd fail and end up a vegetable instead of being done with it all."

"What kind of rope?"

"Clothesline. I read it was the strongest out there for this kind of thing."

"There's books about how to…you know, I mean do they show pictures or anything? That just seems weird."

"On the computer," I said. "Message boards and stuff."

"Huh."

I waited for him to say something else but he seemed to be falling back to sleep. There was certainly the chance he could choke in his sleep—I'd heard enough cautionary tales about rock stars and popular teenagers choking to death on vomit when they were passed out—but that seemed like a long shot and would take more time than I was prepared to invest in this. I picked up the shotgun again and pointed it at his chest, trying to imagine the scene at the Carter house where he and his brother gunned down two guys in cold blood.

But Jay hadn't killed anyone. Not that I saw at least. Not then. But what about the bloodbath at Posey's office? I'd assumed he did that, but what if it was Posey? Jesus. Was my wife a murderer?

I swung the shotgun up so it was pointed at his head instead of his chest. He was hiding from something, that was pretty obvious. Maybe I would be doing him a favor by killing him before someone nastier got a hold of him. Would I have to kill myself though too? Would Posey torture me? I turned the gun on myself and pressed it against the bottom of my jaw then slid it down to my chest. Where would be the best place to fire so it would be quick? While I ran various scenarios through my head, Jay came back to life with a spark and he reached out for the gun in my hands. Instincts I didn't even know I had kicked in and I snapped the stock of the gun into his face, knocking him back to the ground. He wasn't moving at all now and was bleeding from his nose and mouth.

A phone somewhere in the trailer rang loudly enough to rattle my insides and almost made me pull the trigger. It was so loud I thought for sure it was ringing right next to me, but I didn't see a phone anywhere in the kitchen. I followed the sound as best as I could out of the kitchen and through the living room into the back of the house. There was a small bedroom to my left paneled in the same 1980s basement style as the hallway with a small pressboard dresser and two sets of wooden bunk beds the only furnishings of note. There was another bedroom at the back of the trailer with the door closed, but I didn't need to check that bedroom because the ringing was coming from the bathroom to my left. I peeked in and saw the reason it was so loud: there was a giant payphone hanging over the toilet. I answered it.

"Where's Jay?"

It sounded like Posey's voice.

"Who is this?"

"Come on, Dom, I saw you in the driveway. What did you do to him?"

"I took him out."

I heard her gasp. Posey never gasped. She was always in control of her emotions. If she seemed like she was letting loose or showing emotion, it was calculated. But that gasp sounded real. It sounded like she believed me.

"What's your next move?"

"We were drinking, him and I, and he told me some things about you. About what you did back at the office."

"Come on, Dom, you know me. He was desperate. He was trying to save himself."

"How did you find this place? Nobody is supposed to know about it."

"Jay's never been good about keeping secrets."

"What do you want, Posey?"

"I need your help."

I hung up. I knew she'd call back and I knew I'd eventually say yes. But I wanted to make a point and I had to take the opportunities when they presented themselves. The phone rang again and I grabbed it on the first ring. I wanted to make her wait but I was curious and yes, that was probably going to kill me.

"Stop being a jerk," she said. "Lindsey's hurt and we need

someplace to lay low."

"What happened?"

This time she hung up on me. I wanted to hate her. I certainly didn't trust her. But I was looking forward to seeing her. Before she showed up I needed to get Jay out of the kitchen. As much as I hated the sudden insecurity of it, I left the shotgun on the couch so I could use both of my hands to better handle Jay. He snorted when I grabbed him under the arms and I waited to see if he would move at all, but he remained limp and virtually impossible to move. When dragging didn't work, I tried pushing him and tried lifting him from the torso and couldn't find any way to leverage my weakling writer body enough to move his stocky and loaded frame more than a token distance.

I was just about to look through the cabinets for some kind of rope to tie and drag him with when I heard a car coming up the driveway. There was no time to move him so I did the next best thing and ran out to the living room to grab the blanket off of the couch and threw it over him just as the car outside was pulling up to the house. I got back to the couch and grabbed the shotgun then waited for Posey to come through the door. It wasn't long before she kicked the door open and pushed her way in with a conscious Lindsey propped on her shoulder. Lindsey was bloody all over, but the worst of it seemed to be concentrated in the area of her stomach where Posey was holding a shirt I recognized as an old Detroit State University football sweatshirt of her brother's she kept in the office. I wasn't sure if the symbolism of it keeping Lindsey alive was intentional, but I found it amusing anyway.

"Get over here and help me," Posey yelled.

I did and left the shotgun on the couch behind me. This really wasn't in my wheelhouse at all, but I was still embarrassed by the move when I looked back at the couch and saw it.

"What happened?"

"Not now, Dominick. Just get her on the couch."

I backed away from them and reclaimed the shotgun.

"Not until you tell me what happened. Did you shoot her?"

"Jesus, Dom."

No, she didn't answer the question, in case you're paying attention. I looked at Lindsey for her reaction. She shook her head no.

"The other one," Lindsey groaned before falling to the ground.

"I thought you said Jay killed his brother."

"Pick her up. *Please*."

I squatted down and wrapped Lindsey's arms around my neck and carried her over to the couch and propped her up in the corner furthest away from the kitchen, making it less likely, hopefully, that anyone would look in there in the short term. Posey leaned down and tended to the towel before turning back to me.

"Go get me a—"

"I'm not your fucking nurse," I said. "I'm barely your husband. Tell me what happened to her."

"Charlie Taylor shot her. He walked into my office, pointed his gun at me, and then shot her."

"Why was she there in the first place? Why was Charlie there? Why in the hell were *you* still there?"

Lindsey groaned and gurgled and drew Posey's attention back to her. It looked like Posey might make a move on her own and I realized that likely meant her going into the kitchen so I headed off that instinct and went into the kitchen myself.

"I need some alcohol and more towels from that back cabinet," she said.

I grabbed a bottle of vodka and a bottle of gin from the table and tossed them to her like we used to do when we were first living together and we'd have drunken taco night. I was about to miss her again when I had a different thought.

"How do you know where the towels are?"

"I'm really not trying to be a bitch here, Dom. I know you've got a lot of questions and I've been shit about keeping you in the loop. But right now I need to help Lindsey out and you need to figure out which stream of questioning you want to berate me with."

Blaming it on me again. My bad timing and lack of focus rather than her secrets and backstabbing.

"Fuck this," I said, feeling my confidence grow as I stormed out of the trailer and slammed the door behind me, even as my stomach quivered.

Posey followed me out and yelled at me

"Come on, don't be stupid."

"You three can rot here for all I care."

A pause while the light bulb went off over her head.

"What do you mean three of us?"

"You knew I didn't kill him," I said. "He's passed out on the kitchen floor under the big blanket."

I wanted to leave on a quip or something witty, but was at a loss and more concerned with maximizing the escape opportunity. And then she dragged me back in.

"You're right," she said, standing on the porch like a redneck pope delivering a hillbilly homily. "I shot them. I didn't want to. It was a mess. They weren't who I thought they were."

"Why?"

"Don't make me say it. I know you're smart enough to figure it out even if you don't believe it."

"You're not putting this on me again. I want to hear it from your—"

"I killed them to save myself," she said. "To save my family."

"To take over your family."

"The family business. Yes. And I need your help. You're in this whether you want to be or not, so pick your side."

"You or Charlie?"

"It shouldn't even be a choice. Not after what we've been through."

"I'm not the disease," I said. "You are."

"Make your choice, Dominick. And make it quick."

I went back inside to live or die with my gangster wife.

"We need to get Jay up," Posey said, resuming control of the shit show. "We need his help."

"His brother is coming here? Did he follow you?"

"I don't know. Maybe he doesn't know about this place."

"Then we're safe? We can't just wait for him if he's not coming."

"He's coming."

"But you just said you don't know for sure—"

"Goddammit, Dominick, cut the questions and—"

"No," I screamed, stepping into her body and getting right in her face. "You said you needed me. If that's true, then you have to trust me. Give me information. Trust me with it and trust me to make my own decisions."

"You're a body," she said. "Do you like that truth? You're cannon fodder; something to distract Charlie when he shows up here while I do what I need to do."

"Which is kill him?"

"And you're not going to do it. Which is fine. It's who you are. Hopefully nothing happens to you. Despite your troubles and the messes you leave behind—"

"The messes *I* leave behind?"

"You have a survival instinct that is amazing. You'll live through this. I have no doubt of that. But what do you want when this is over?"

"Lindsey's bleeding to death over there, one of your best friends, allegedly, is choking on his own vomit in the kitchen, and you're asking me to think about my future?"

"Seems like the perfect time to me. What do you want, Dominick? From me. From life. From yourself. Do you just want to keep surviving and moving on to the next crisis or do you want to be proactive?"

I always thought crises were supposed to galvanize a person's thoughts and life plan. That's what the movies always tell us. Any story for that matter. Tragedy and obstacles befall a character in limbo and they are changed through those events. My story was certainly applying the needed pressure, but what changes were being made? I was certainly a different person. But was I a better person? Was I closer to achieving my goals in life? Hell, was I closer to figuring out what my goals in life were?

I backed away from her and slumped my body in defeat.

"I don't know."

"Then you lose," she said.

"You don't get to determine the timetable of my life. These aren't my only options."

"Right now they are. You put yourself in these situations, not me. When you blow enough of life's good opportunities you'll find yourself left with your choice of bad opportunities."

"Was I a good opportunity you blew?"

"Don't do that to yourself, Dom."

Our enlightening conversation was cut short by the echoing ring of the bathroom payphone.

"He's here," she said. "Make your choice."

In my head I envisioned a backwoods version of *Home Alone* where we would set a series of inventive traps to defend the trailer against the approaching enemy, but Posey had a different idea. She ran into the kitchen and pulled the ugly yellow stove away from the wall and shook it back and forth until I heard the hiss of the gas line breaking loose. Ignoring Jay's sprawled body on the floor, she grabbed the Johnny Walker Red bottle and came back my way.

I made my choice, sprinting to the couch to grab the shotgun before she got to me. There will never be a way to know for absolute certain that she was going to knock me out and blow me up with the others, but I made my choice and I had no problem defending it.

I shot once and hit her in the chest then quickly pumped the second shell in and shot her again, hitting her lower in the torso. She fell to the ground with a look of shock on her face that should have made me happy—I'd surprised her and done something she didn't think I was capable of—but all I felt was sick and depressed.

There was no time to dwell on that though. I had enough of an adrenaline boost to provide me the strength needed to drag Lindsey first out of the trailer and into the driveway and then Jay. My chest and arms were burning and my legs kept seizing up on me toward the end, but I got both of them out of the house and even had Lindsey propped up in the front passenger's seat when I heard another vehicle approaching. True to the Taylor family having vehicles I wouldn't expect, Charlie was approaching in a giant late model burgundy conversion van. I quickened my pace to get Jay into the car but the adrenaline was quickly wearing off, making that nearly impossible. When I did finally get him squished into the backseat, I noticed the van was still where it had been the last time I looked. Could it be tourists rather than Charlie? The van would make a whole lot more sense driven by a beleaguered dad rather than a homicidal corrections guard. If it was tourists, where was Charlie? The answer came quickly when a man got out of the van who looked sort of like Charlie, though it was hard to tell for sure because he had on jeans and a black T-shirt instead of his uniform. When he reached back into the van and came out with a giant assault rifle and pointed it at me, I knew it was him.

The shotgun was still inside but I'd used up the two shells Jay had loaded it with and I wasn't sure if there were any more in the car anywhere. My best shot, as I saw it, was to use the biggest, strongest, fastest weapon at my disposal: the Volvo.

I jumped into the driver's seat and it wasn't until I went to start the car that I realized I didn't have the keys. I glanced up at the rearview mirror to see how quickly Charlie was approaching, but he was still in the same spot he'd been in. Was he waiting for me? Trying to intimidate me?

Shit. Jay's pockets. That's where the keys were.

I got back out of the car to try and get into the back seat when three shots whizzed by me, forcing me quickly back inside the car. The only way into the backseat without getting shot was to scramble between the driver's seat and the passenger's seat and roll into the back onto Jay's lap. The keys were in his front pocket and took a few tugs before coming free. It took a few extra tries to get back into the driver's seat and upright before I started the car. Lindsey was coming back to life and moaning while trying to sit up in her seat.

"Head shot," she said.

"All I have is the shotgun. And I don't think there's any more ammo for it around."

"Him. You. That's..."

"That's why he's waiting?"

She nodded.

"He wants to shoot me in the head when I try and drive by him?"

Another nod.

"So what do I do?"

"Decoy."

"I don't get what that means."

She gurgled a bit and slumped back down in her seat.

I had no idea what she meant but I didn't see any options other than backing down the driveway as fast as I could and hope he missed. A shot to the head would be clean at least so I wouldn't feel it.

Reverse.

Foot on the gas.

Shit. Shit. Shit.

I kept my eye on Charlie in the mirror and saw him raise the gun up.

It would have been easier for him if I was driving directly at him. My hope was his trying to aim through the entire back of the station wagon and still get a clean hit would work to my advantage. Lindsey gurgled something but I couldn't understand what it was. As I got closer to Charlie I started turning the wheel to drive around him and Lindsey gurgled again, this time louder, but still unintelligible. She shifted in her seat and finally dragged herself fully upright.

"Duck," she said, grabbing the wheel.

I didn't duck; I didn't have time. She pulled the steering wheel violently toward her and then her head exploded. Glass shattered, and brains and blood splattered the windshield and me and the rest of the car. The car started getting away from me so I pulled the wheel back toward me without looking in the mirror and shook it back and forth enough to stop the car from flipping over then felt a hard jerk as my body flew forward before being caught by my seatbelt. The car came to a stop and I finally ducked.

I kept my head down and opened my door, trying to get out of the car without providing another chance for Charlie to take a shot at me. Deep down I knew I was safe, knew I had run him over with the car, knew Lindsey had been my hero, but I didn't relax until I saw Charlie's body pinned under the Volvo. His gun was on the ground next to him and I picked it up without hesitation. I told myself the first time I shot him that it was to put him out of his misery. The second shot was for Lindsey. Then I emptied the clip into him because he was an asshole.

# EPILOGUE

I was under suspicion for a long time from the police, who were certain I was smarter than I appeared and that I was a more vital key to the Taylor family criminal syndicate than I was. The Taylor family also kept a close watch on me in case I was preparing to take Posey's role as heir apparent, but a lawyer who owed me a favor eventually talked some sense into Jay and convinced him to tell the judge what he needed to hear and then to hire me as his ghostwriter to tell the rest of the world everything else. My boss never filed the paperwork for me to be officially terminated from my job at the university so I still had platinum insurance that paid for the obscene amount of therapy I was under. The time I spent in jail was good for me, and I made notes for a short story that would add a level of authenticity new to my work.

That story was eventually published by the same website that had published some of my earlier stories, but instead of dying on the vine like the others it was picked up for the *Best*

*American Mystery Stories* anthology the next year and nominated for an Edgar Allan Poe Award from the Mystery Writers of America. I was currently working on expanding it into a novel.

The day they finally released me from the psych ward, I got the invitation in the mail for the Edgar Awards banquet in March. I was finally going to get to New York City. I needed a date and everyone close to me was dead, so I showed up at Parker's house and asked him if he'd like to go with me. He waffled back and forth so I handed over a piece of paper my lawyer had given me.

"If you don't go with me, I'll have to take Titus Wade."

"That doesn't make any sense."

He looked down at the paper when I didn't answer him and then said, "You're disgusting, you know that?"

"I've been awarded full custody of my brother-in-law's final legacy," I said. "I just want to make sure I don't ever lose that sample again."

"All that money you got from your wife's estate to do whatever you want with and you blew it getting custody of a load of sperm?"

"What can I say? I'm a romantic."

He laughed it off and so did I, but it wasn't true. I was petty and vindictive and my optimism was starting to crack under the weight of everything I'd been through. I couldn't bring myself to say it out loud, but the real reason I wanted Parker to go with me was because I didn't trust myself in New York City alone. I'd moved beyond being a danger to myself; my therapist had done some amazing things to help me work through my guilt, my trauma, and the reality of the awful things I'd done.

I'm not innocent. Not anymore, if there even was a time I

ever was. But I was worried about what I was capable of against other people. I still got twitchy around crowds and my patience for loud noises was minimal at best. I'd come close to hurting a lot of people before Posey finally cracked me and now that it had been unleashed, I was trying my best to keep it under control and a giant city full of noise and emotional stimulants didn't seem like the best place to be alone at the moment.

"I appreciate the offer, son, I really do, but you don't look well and I'm not sure I should be encouraging you to do something that stupid."

I nodded and took a deep breath.

"I feel great," I said.

And I really meant it. Right then. For that moment.

"That's good to hear. But it sounds like you have some… you've got some responsibilities here with your new inheritance. Maybe we can go later when it's quieter, you know?"

It was funny to hear Parker Farmington lost for words and better yet lost for words around me. I had no idea what he was feeling inside and what the extent of his loss of and grief for Lindsey was, but I felt drawn to him as seemed to be habit while recovering from getting into trouble.

"I couldn't let it go to some stranger," I said. "So much blood was spilled over that sample and what it represented. It can't go to someone who would have no idea what they were in for.'

"That's smart. It's good of you to do that."

"It represents a lot," I said. "About me. My lawyer helped me get custody and find a nice private storage facility where I can visit whenever I want."

This time it was his turn to nod sadly. I suspected he was thinking about visiting Lindsey if that was possible.

"She saved my life," I said. "I told you that, right?"

"Are you going to make it a life worth saving?"

I shrugged.

"I hope so."

# Acknowledgements

While fewer people helped me bring this book into the world than the last one, the effort required of this crew was far, far more trying. So I offer my deepest thanks to my support team. You've saved me untold millions in therapy bills and court costs. First and always are Dave White and Sarah Weinman who answer every panicked email, every gossipy email, and every stupid email with a charm and maturity I envy. In a close second are Jon Jordan, Ruth Jordan, Judy Bobalik, Michael Koryta, Laura Lippman, Paul Guyot, John Rickards, Frank Wheeler, Maria Wheeler, Karen Olson, Chris Holm, Katrina Holm, Holly West, Alison Dasho, Patti Abbott, Jay Stringer, Dan Malmon, Kate Malmon, Bryan VanMeter, Alex Segura, and yes, even Rob Hart. Jason Pinter, as always, deserves a hearty shout-out for making my dreams come true again.

Finally, my wife Becky and my kids Spenser, Holly, and Natalie make this all worth it. I love you guys so much.

# About the Author

Bryon Quertermous is the author of MURDER BOY available from Polis Books. He was born and raised in Michigan His short stories have appeared in *Plots With Guns, Thuglit,* an *Crime Factory,* among others, and in the anthologies *Hardcor Hardboiled, The Year's Finest Crime, Mystery Stories,* and *Uncag Me.* He was shortlisted for the prestigious Debut Dagger Awar from the U.K. Crime Writers' Association. He currently live outside of Detroit with his wife and three children. Visit him a bryonquertermous.com and follow him on Twitter at @BryonQ